THE
LAST
SUSPICIOUS
HOLDOUT

Also by Ladee Hubbard

The Rib King

The Talented Ribkins

THE
LAST
SUSPICIOUS
HOLDOUT

STORIES

LADEE
HUBBARD

AMISTAD
— *35* —

An Imprint of HarperCollins*Publishers*

The following stories were originally published in these publications:

"Bitch: An Etymology of Family Values," *Transition*, no. 128, 2019
"False Cognates," *Guernica*, March 2018
"Five People Who Crave Sauce," *Oxford American*, Summer 2021
"Flip Lady," *GUD*, Spring 2009
"The Night Nurses," *Callaloo*, Fall 2017
"Paulie Sparks," *Copper Nickel*, Spring 2018
"There He Go," *Rosebud*, Summer 2013
"Trash," *Crab Orchard Review*, Fall 2011
"Yams," *Virginia Quarterly Review*, Summer 2018

HarperCollins books may be purchased for educational, business, or sales promotional use. For information, please email the Special Markets Department at SPsales@harpercollins.com.

FIRST EDITION

Designed by Nancy Singer

Library of Congress Cataloging-in-Publication Data has been applied for.

ISBN 978-0-06-297909-4

22 23 24 25 26 LSC 10 9 8 7 6 5 4 3 2 1

Contents

THE
LAST
SUSPICIOUS
HOLDOUT

Flip Lady

(1992)

1.

History:

Raymond Brown hears the sound of laughter. He puts down his book and looks out the window.

Here they come now, children of the ancient ones, the hewers of wood, the cutters of cane barreling down the sidewalk on their Huffys and Schwinns. Little legs pumping over fat rubber tires, brakes squealing as they pull into the drive, standing on tiptoes as they straddle their bikes and stare at the house with their mouths hanging open.

Just like before. Some of them he still recognizes. He made out with that girl's sister in the seventh grade, played basketball with that boy's uncle in high school. This one was all right until his brother joined the army, that one was okay until her daddy went to jail. And you see that girl in the back? The chubby one standing by the curb, next to the brand-new Schwinn? She hasn't been the same since the invasion of Grenada, nine years ago, in 1983.

The Spice Island. When the Marines landed, she was three years old, living in St. George's near the medical clinic with her mother, the doctor and Aunt Ruby, the nurse. The power went off, the hospital plunging into blue darkness while machine gunfire cackled in the distance like a bag of Jiffy Pop bubbling up on a stove. *Oh no*, Aunt Ruby said. *Just like before*.

It's all there, in the book on his lap. Colonizers fanning out across the Atlantic like a hurricane, not exactly hungry but looking for spice. They claimed the land, they built the plantations, they filled the Americas up with slaves. Sugar kept the workers happy, distracted them from grief. And four hundred years later you have your military invasions and McDonald's Happy Meals, your Ho Hos and preemptive strikes. Your Oreos and Reaganomics, your Cap'n Crunch.

And Kool-Aid. These kids can't get enough of it. They sit in the driveway, they shift in their seats, they grip the plastic streamers affixed to their handlebars. One of them kicks a kickstand and steps forward, fingers curled into a small tight fist as he knocks on the kitchen door.

"Flip Lady? You in there?"

Just like before. They roamed the entire earth in search of spice so why not here, why not now?

"Flip Lady? You home? It's me, Calvin. . . ."

For the past few weeks they've been coming almost every day.

Raymond closes the curtain. He shakes his head and turns towards the darkness of the back bedroom. "Mama? It's those fucking kids again."

2.

The squeak of old mattress coils, a single bang of a headboard against a bedroom wall. The Flip Lady wills herself upright, sets her feet on the floor, sits on the edge of her bed and stares at the chipped polish on her left big toe. She stands up, reaches for her slippers, straightens out her green housedress, and walks out the bedroom door.

The Flip Lady shuffles into the living room where her nineteen-year-old son, Raymond, sits on a low couch, reading. Long brown body hunched forward, elbows resting on his knees as he peers at the page of the book on his lap. In an instant his life flashes through her mind in a series of fractured images, like a VHS tape on rewind. She sees him at sixteen, face hidden behind a comic book, then at seven when his feet barely touched the floor. And before that as a chubby toddler, gripping the cushions with fat meaty fists, laughing as he hoisted himself onto the couch. Without breaking her stride, and for want of anything else to say, she mutters, "I see you reading," and passes into the kitchen.

The Flip Lady lifts a pickle jar full of loose change from the counter and looks out the kitchen window.

"That you, Calvin?" she says to the little boy standing on her porch.

"Afternoon, ma'am." Calvin smiles.

She twists the lid off the jar, opens the kitchen door, and squints at the multitude assembled in her backyard.

Calvin plunges his hand into his pants pocket and pulls out a fistful of dimes. He drops them into her jar with a series of empty pings.

"Well, all right then," the Flip Lady says.

Calvin glances over his shoulder and winks.

She walks towards her refrigerator while Calvin stands in the doorway. He cocks his head and peers past her into the living room. Glass angel figurines and the tea set on the lace doily in the cabinet against the wall; bronzed baby shoes mounted on a wooden plaque; framed high school graduation photos and Sears portraits of her two sons sitting on top of the TV set; a stack of LPs lined up on the floor. A dark green La-Z-Boy recliner and the plaid couch where her younger son sits with a book on his lap. Calvin turns his head again and sees the Flip Lady standing in the middle of her bright yellow kitchen, easing two muffin trays stuffed with Dixie cups out of her freezer.

The Flip Lady studies Calvin's face as he scoops the cups out of the trays, licking his lips, eyes lit up like birthday candles. She smiles. Her boys were the same way when they were that age, crowding around her back door with all their friends, giddy with excitement as they sucked on her homemade popsicles. She used to hand them out when their friends came over to play after school and on weekends; it was a way to keep them in her backyard where she could watch them from the kitchen window. A good mother, she wanted to get to know how her boys passed their time and with whom. She wanted to memorize their playmates' faces and study their gestures until she felt confident that she could tell the clever from the calculated, the dreamy-eyed from the dangerous, the quiet from the cruel. She hadn't done it for money. No one had to thank her, although her neighbors told her many times how much they appreciated her looking out for their children that way.

The Flip Lady frowns. Of course, everything does change, eventually. There comes a time when a mother has to accept that the promise of sugary sweets has lost its ability to soothe all grief. They don't want your Kool-Aid anymore. They busy, they got other things to do. One day you find yourself standing alone in the kitchen, hand wrapped around a cold cup, melting ice dripping down your fingers as you wonder to yourself when exactly the good little boys standing on your back porch became the big bad men walking out your front door.

She looks at Calvin. "How was school today, son? You studying hard, being a good boy? Doing what your mama tells you?"

"Yes, ma'am." Calvin walks around, passing out Dixie cups to his friends.

"Well, all right then," the Flip Lady says.

3.

What you get for your money is a hunk of purple ice, a Dixie cup full of frozen Kool-Aid. The girl in the back stares at hers. It's not quite what she was expecting, given how far they have come to get it. According to the black plastic Casio attached to her left wrist, they've been riding for a full twenty minutes in the opposite direction from where she was trying to get to, which was home. One minute she was in the schoolyard unlocking her bike and the next they were standing over her, the whole group of them saying, *Come with us*. She knew it wasn't an invitation but an order. They were taking her to wherever it was they went when they sprinted off after class, their laughter echoing in the distance long after they'd disappeared past the school gate. How could she say no? She lifts the cup to her open mouth and runs her tongue along its surface, absorbing flat sweetness and a salty aftertaste.

"It's just Kool-Aid," someone says.

The girl closes her mouth. She looks around the parking lot of Byrdie's Burgers, where they have parked their bikes to eat. Everyone is pushing the bottoms of their cups with the pads of their thumbs, making those sugar lumps rise into the air. They're tilting their cups to the side and pulling them out, melting Kool-Aid dripping down their hands as they flip them over, then carefully placing them back in the cups, bottom sides up. They're sucking on their fingers, they're licking their lips, their mouths pressed against homemade popsicle flips.

"What's the matter? Don't they have Kool-Aid where you come from?"

The girl looks down at her cup. She pushes her thumbs against the bottom but presses too hard; the hunk of purple ice pops out too fast and soars over the rim. She tries to catch it, but her hands fumble; it dribbles down the front of her shirt, then lands with a thud on the pavement.

"Now that's a shame."

The girl wipes her hands on the front of her shorts, palms already sticky. She blames her upbringing, all those years spent stuck on that rock, how to flip a homemade popsicle was just one more thing she should have known. She got the exact same looks from the kids on Grenada, after she moved there with her mother and Aunt Ruby all those years ago: *What you come here for? What you want with this rock, when everybody trying to get off it?* As if only white people were supposed to spin in dizzy circles like that, as missionaries or volunteers or tourists on extended leave. She can still see her former playmates in the eyes of her new school's handful of immigrant kids, with their high-water pants and loud polyester shirts, huddling and whispering to each other as they move down the halls. They look tired, fagged out from the journey, but at least they have an excuse. She's not even West Indian. Everyone knows her uncle Todd lives right around the block from Henry's Bar and has been living there for at least twenty years.

"What a waste."

When her mother said they were moving back to the States she'd been like everyone else she knew, picturing New York or LA like she saw on TV, not some narrow sliver of southern suburbia wedged senselessly in between. Instead she is surrounded by a whole parking lot full of distracted sucking children who don't like her anyway.

"Go get another one," someone says. Calvin, the boss around here, although sometimes they take turns.

"It's only ten cents. Ain't you even got another dime?"

"What's the problem? You scared to go back by yourself?"

"What's the matter? Don't you want one?"

Of course she wants one. But she wants that one there, already dissolving into a pool of purple ooze at her feet. If she can't have it then she wants to go home, sit on the couch, eat leftover Entenmann's cookies from the box, and watch *Star Trek* reruns until her mother gets home from work at the hospital.

She looks back at the Flip Lady's house, now halfway down the block. She's tired of traveling the wrong way, dragging herself in the wrong direction without real rhyme or actual reason. But she also doesn't want to cause trouble, doesn't want to make waves. She reaches for the handlebars of her bike.

"Naw, leave it." They lick their lips and smile. "We'll watch it for you."

But they lie: in a few minutes they are going to teach her a lesson about realness, about keeping it. Because even her accent is fake. Because she rides around on a Schwinn that is just like theirs, except it is brand-new.

"Go on, girl."

Plus, she's fat.

The girl nods her head. She knows they are going to start talking about her as soon as her back is turned. They're a mean bunch; she's seen them do some terrible things at school. She's already figured out that it does no good to wander in and out of earshot of this group. Either you've got to stay knuckle to knuckle, packed tight like a fist, or else give them a wide berth and do all you can to not draw attention to yourself.

She turns around and starts walking. She can hear them whispering and laughing behind her, a hot humid jungle of bad moods circling her footsteps, gathering in strength with each step she takes. A flash of fear tickles her nose, like when you're swimming and accidentally inhale water. But she does not stop walking, somehow convinced that to turn around midstride will only make things worse.

She knocks on the Flip Lady's door, expecting to see the kind face of the woman who answered it not a half hour before. Instead it's a man, dressed in a pair of sweatpants and a blue T-shirt, a little brown Chihuahua shivering in the palm of his left hand. She stares up at flaring nostrils, dark eyes, eyebrows arched.

"What do you want?"

"I dropped mine."

Raymond shakes his head. "No. I'm not doing this. Mama's not here. Understand? Flip Lady gone. She went out. Shopping. To buy more Kool-Aid, most likely. So why don't you just come back tomorrow. . . ."

A harsh peel of laughter cuts across the horizon. The girl puts her head down and reaches into her pocket. She holds out a dime like a peace offering.

Raymond recoils. "I don't want that. What am I supposed to do with that? Girl, you better just go on home."

He squints into the distance behind her. "Those your friends? Little heathens . . ."

The girl hears the harsh scrape of metal against concrete as the man steps past her, onto the porch.

"Hey, girl. Is that your bike?"

She winces at the sound of rubber soles pounding on the spokes and stares down at the mat in front of the door.

"Hey, girl . . . What the heck are they doing—"

She shuts her eyes, feels a stiff pressure in her groin, like a sudden swift kick against her bladder, then a sharp tingling sensation between her legs.

"Hey, girl, turn around. . . ."

The girl looks up. "May I use your bathroom please?"

RAYMOND LOOKS AT THE CHILD breathing hard with her thighs clamped together, shifting her weight from side to side. He bites his lip then nods and points down the hall, watches her sprint past his friend Tony, who is standing in the middle of the living room grinning from ear to ear.

"You from Jamaica?" Tony says as the girl rushes past. She runs into the bathroom and slams the door.

Raymond shakes his head. It's all there, in his book, he thinks. It's always the weak and the homely who get left behind. Stranded on the back porch, knees shaking as they quiver and dance, thin rivers of pee running down their ashy legs.

4.

The girl sits on the toilet in a pink-tiled bathroom, staring at a stack of *Ebony* and *Newsweek* magazines in a brass rack near the sink. She's thinking about her bike, about how much she's going to miss it. She's only had it for a few weeks, but still. It's something she begged and pleaded for, something she swore she needed to fit in at her new school. Now she doesn't even want to look at it. A few minutes before the Flip Lady's son knocked on the door and told her he would fix it so she can ride home, but it's too late. It's already ruined. She's already peed herself and run away.

Everybody's always so busy running, so busy trying to save their own skins, she remembers her aunt Ruby telling her. *That's what's wrong with this world. We've got to stand together if we're going to stand at all.* The girl had liked the sound of that even if she sensed that it didn't really apply to her. She'd seen her aunt and mother working in the clinic, stood numb and mystified by the deliberateness with which they thrust themselves into other people's wounds. Stitching a cut, dressing a burn, giving a shot, connecting an IV. It was intimidating, the steadiness of her mother's hand sometimes. Even now, in the midst of grief. Like some nights when her mother stomped into the living room and cut off the TV in the middle of the evening news, her voice damming the flood of silence that followed with the simple statement: "They lie."

The girl reaches for the roll of toilet paper and wipes off the insides of her legs. She pulls up her damp panties and zips her shorts. When she opens the door she finds Tony alone in the living room, crouched down on the floor, peering behind the stack of LPs lined up against the wall.

"You feeling better?"

When she doesn't say anything, he puts the records back. He stands up, shoves his hands into his pockets, and smiles.

"So, what, you from Jamaica?"

The girl shakes her head. "I come from here."

"Not talking like that you don't." Tony walks past her and then stops. He crosses his arms in front of his chest, puts one hand on his chin and stares down at the couch.

"I lived on Grenada for a time but—"

"What's that?"

She watches as he kneels in front of the couch. He lifts the cushion and runs his hand underneath it like he's looking for spare change.

"Another island," she says.

He puts the cushion back and sits on top of it, bouncing up and down a few times to force the cushion back into place.

Tony nods. "Y'all smoke a lot of ganja down there too?"

The girl shrugs awkwardly. She wonders what about her appearance might remind this man of a Rastafarian. Rastafarians wore dusty clothes, had calloused feet and thick clumps of matted hair. They sat in the waiting room, making the clinic smell like salt and homemade lye soap. Her mother checked their charts while Aunt Ruby rubbed their arms with cotton pads dipped in alcohol. When they saw the needle, Aunt Ruby smiled and told them it was just a pinprick. *Don't worry, it will be all right*, she promised. *Just look at me.*

But, no, she didn't smoke a lot of ganja.

"That's all right," Tony says. "You still got that sweet accent, huh?" He pulls a bouquet of plastic flowers out of a white vase, peers down inside it, and holds the flowers up to his nose.

"I like things sweet." Tony puts the flowers back in the vase and reaches underneath the table, running his hand along the wood panels underneath. The girl stares down at the books stacked on top of it. And next to the table is an open cardboard box with still more books tucked inside.

The kitchen door swings open. Raymond walks back into the living room, tossing a wrench onto the table, next to the books.

"How far away you live?" He can already see her starting to blink rapidly. "I mean, I tried. But the body's all bent. You're going to have to just carry it or drag it or something, I don't know. . . ."

"Damn." Tony shakes his head. "What's wrong with these fucking kids today? Why you think they so evil?"

Raymond looks at the girl: short, stiff plaits of hair standing up at the back of her neck, dirty white T-shirt with a pink ladybug appliqué stretched across the stomach, plaid shorts, socks spattered with purple Kool-Aid stains. He used to feel sorry for awkward, homely girls like that. But now sometimes he thinks maybe they are really better off. "I tried."

"Why they do that to you, girl?" Tony says. She just stands there, hands clasped behind her back, swaying from side to side.

"You gonna be all right?" Raymond nods towards the front door. "You want a glass of water or something, before you go?"

"Hey, Ray, man, you remember us? You remember back in the day?"

Raymond shrugs. All he knows is that the girl is not moving. She just stands there staring down at the stack of books on the table.

"I think we were just as bad," Tony says.

"Let me get you that glass of water." Raymond disappears into the kitchen. The cabinet squeaks open, followed by the sound of crushed ice crumbling into a glass.

"And your mama with them flips," Tony yells from the living room. "When'd she start up with that again? I haven't seen those things in years."

"Well, you're lucky," Raymond calls back. Just thinking about all those little kids crowding around his mama's yard is enough to make him wince. She started making those fucking popsicles again almost as soon as he came back to hold her hand at his brother Sam's funeral. He's convinced there is something wrong with it, that it is unhealthy somehow, an unnatural distraction from grief. And look at the kind of hassles it leads to. He puts the glass under the faucet and pours the girl her water. All he wants is to get the child out of his house before she has time to pee herself again.

"When did she start charging people?" Tony asks. Raymond closes his eyes and shuts the water off. He knows Tony doesn't mean anything by it but, really, that's the part that bothers him the most, all those jars of fucking dimes. He walks back into the living room.

"Man." Raymond shakes his head. He hands the girl her water. "I don't want to talk about fucking Kool-Aid."

Tony shrugs. He looks at the girl.

"They used to be free."

5.

There are too many people in the house, Raymond thinks. That's what the problem is. He can sense that, Tony and the girl filling up the space, making him feel crowded and cramped. For the past five days it's been just him and the books, the box he found hidden in the back of his brother's closet. And it shocked him because he'd never actually seen his brother read anything more substantial than a comic book. But he knew they were his brother's books and that his brother actually read them because he recognized the handwriting scribbled in the margins on almost every page.

The girl lowers her glass and nods her head towards the stack on the table. "Are all those yours?" she asks Raymond.

"Naw." He shakes his head. "They belong to someone else."

"Just a little light reading to pass the time, huh, Ray?" Tony says.

He picks up a book and glances down at the cover, assessing its weight. "Looks dry."

Raymond shuts his eyes. The word "fool" bubbles up in his mind involuntarily, before he can force it back down with guilt. He's known Tony for twelve years, ever since they both got assigned the same homeroom teacher in the second grade. Somehow, when Raymond went to college, he'd imagined himself missing Tony a lot more than he actually had. He opens his eyes and looks at the girl.

"Why did you ask me that? About the books? I mean, what difference does it make to you who they belong to?"

She points to the one lying open. "I know that one."

"What do you mean you know it?"

"I mean I've seen it. I read it."

"That thick-ass book?" Tony glances down at it, then back up at the girl. "Naw. Really?"

"Parts of it," the girl says. "Aunt Ruby gave it to me."

"Now you see that?" Tony says. "Another one with the books. Now we got two. . . ." He stands up and walks to the kitchen.

Raymond squints at the girl in front of him, rocking slowly from side to side as she drinks her glass of water.

"Look, girl. You've been here for almost an hour now. What's the problem? Don't you want to go home?" He studies her face. "Are you scared? Worried your daddy is going to beat you or something, for letting them fuck your bike up like that?"

"I don't have a daddy."

"Then what is it?"

"It's the bike." The girl shakes her head, lower lip popping out in a pout. "I don't want it."

"What do you mean you don't want it?" He winces at the sudden loud clatter of pots and pans being pushed aside in one of his mother's kitchen drawers.

"You don't want to take it home?"

The girl nods.

"Well, leave it then. You just go home and I'll keep it in the garage and you can come back for it later, like when Mama's here or something."

A drawer slams shut in the kitchen.

"Hey, man, what are you doing in there?" Raymond yells.

"Where she keep it?"

"What?"

"The Kool-Aid. I'm thirsty."

Raymond frowns. "I told you she went to the store," he yells back. "What the fuck is the matter with you?"

Tony steps back into the living room, squints at Ray.

"There is no fucking Kool-Aid in this house," Raymond says.

"I hear you." Tony nods. He frowns. "Just relax. Hear me? Don't lose your cool."

Tony keeps his eyes locked on Raymond's as he walks backwards to the kitchen, then disappears behind the door.

Raymond looks at the girl.

"I'm trying to be nice."

6.

Tony stands in the middle of a bright yellow kitchen, staring at the dimes in the pickle jar on the windowsill, thinking about Raymond losing his cool. Baby brother is clearly not well. Tony could see that as soon as he walked into the house, sensed it just from talking to Ray on the phone. Something about his big brother, Sam, having all those books in his closet really tripped Ray up for some reason. Maybe Ray forgot other people could read, had a right to read a fucking book when they felt like it.

Ray just needs to get out of the house for a little while, Tony thinks.

Ray just needs some fresh air. Have a beer, smoke some weed, take a walk around the neighborhood and relax. Tony has it all laid out in his mind, the speech he's going to give Ray about how fucked up everything is, how Ray needs to get back up to school before it's too late. *Anybody who likes reading books as much as you do needs to be getting a college education, can't be fucking up a chance like this.* He'll shake his head and tell Ray he understands wanting to be here for your mama and all, but sometimes you got to just put shit aside and go for yours because *how you supposed to help anybody else if you can't even help yourself?* Sam would have wanted him to say all that. Would have said, *Listen to Tony, you know Tony got plenty of sense, always has.*

He's going to tell Ray about how proud of him Sam always was. Tell him that as much as Sam rolled his eyes, everybody could see how much he liked saying it. *Naw, that doofy herb ain't here no more. He up at school.* The eye-rolling was just reflex. *My baby brother, up at college . . .* He'll make up a little lie about how one night he and Sam actually talked about it, tell Ray how ashamed Sam was for hitting him, especially that last time. Knocked his books on the floor, slapped Ray across the face. *Now pick it up.* And really there was something pitiful about it, big man like Sam hitting a little boy like Ray. Tony could see that even then.

But of course, Tony wasn't the one getting slapped. Tony was the one standing on the sidelines watching, the one who had his hands out when it was over. The one who dusted him off, handed him back his book, said *Here you go, Ray* and *Damn, that motherfucker is mean.* And Ray cut his eyes and said, *Oh, that son of a bitch is probably just high, he don't even know what planet he's on half the time,* which Tony knew wasn't true. But he let Ray say it because it made him stop crying and sometimes people just say things.

Tony spins around, opens the door to the pantry. Ray's mama has got all kinds of shit in there: baked beans, Vienna sausages, Del Monte canned peaches, SPAM, a half-full jar of Folgers crystals that has probably been sitting there for years. Tony sucks his teeth, thinking how his grandma is the same way. Can't throw anything out, no matter how nasty or old. Jars of flour, baking powder, baking soda, cornstarch, cornmeal, sugar. He can see how someone might get confused in a pantry like that. If they were crazy, say, or couldn't smell nothing because their nose was too stuffed up from crying all the time.

Ray's mother is not taking very good care of herself these days. That's what Tony's mother said when he told her he was going out to visit Ray: *Saw her shuffling around the supermarket the other day, poor thing with her wig on all crooked and walking around in that nasty house-dress. Just grieving, poor thing. She not taking very good care of herself these days, looks like.* If Tony's mother hadn't pointed it out to him, he might not have even noticed. To him, Ray's mama just looks old. But she always looked like that, even when they were kids.

Tony stands there for a minute, looking up at a jar of what appears to be powdered sugar. He glances over his shoulder and decides that if Ray walks in and asks him what he's doing he'll just shrug and tell him he's got a sweet tooth. He twists the top off the jar and opens a drawer near the sink, looking for something to put it in. He is pulling out a plastic Ziploc bag when he hears a knock on the front door.

He walks back into the living room and sees Raymond peeking out the front window.

"I told you, man," Tony says. "It's the changing of the guard."

Raymond nods. "Just wait here. . . ."

7.

The girl watches Raymond walk out the front door and shut it behind him. She puts her glass of water on the table and stands by the window. She sees Raymond heading out to a car parked by the curb. An arm spills out of the driver's-side window and it is a man's arm, thick and muscular, fingers outstretched to clasp Raymond's hand. Suddenly Raymond looks different to her: thin and awkward, like a boy.

"That's his brother Sam's friend, Sean." Tony shakes his head and sits down on the couch. "Everybody's cool now, but let's see how long that lasts."

Another man's hand appears, dangling out of the rear window, holding out a forty-ounce bottle of beer.

"Somehow they got it in their stupid heads that Sam took something that belonged to them and hid it somewhere, maybe right here in his mama's house."

The girl watches Raymond take the bottle, twist off the cap, and spill a sip onto the pavement before raising it to his lips.

"And you know what's fucked up? I mean really fucked up? I'm starting to think that too."

When the girl turns around, Tony is staring at her from the couch. He lowers his eyes, looks down at the book.

"Hey. You really read this? For real?"

The girl nods. "Aunt Ruby gave it to me."

"Well, who the hell is Aunt Ruby?"

"Mama's friend. She came down with us to Grenada, as part of the Creative Unity Brigade."

Tony picks up the book. Somehow this makes sense to him. Of course there is a Creative Unity Brigade. Somewhere. Full of the righteous, marching proudly, two by two, with their fists in the air. The book is a call to action; he can tell that just by looking at the cover.

"That why y'all moved down there, to that island? Help the needy, feed the poor? That kind of shit? What, you part of a church group or something?"

"Not really."

He flips the book over and stares at the back cover. Outside he can hear the revving of a motor, music blaring through the car's open windows, the screech of brakes as it pulls away from the curb.

"Why did you stop?" he asks the girl. "I mean, why did you all come back?"

The girl stares at him. She has to think for a moment about how to answer because in truth, no one ever asks her that. They ask why she went but never why she came back. Most people she has met here don't even know where Grenada is, except when they sometimes say, *Didn't we already bomb the shit out of that place years ago?* And everyone who hears about the Brigade seems to assume that it was bound to fail simply because it did.

"Aunt Ruby. She gone now."

"Gone where?"

"In the kitchen. She take a bottle of pills."

Tony turns away from her. Tries to picture the woman, Aunt Ruby, but can't. So instead he thinks about Sam, someone he had known all his life, someone he loved, truly. He rises to his feet and as he walks across the room he thrusts an abrupt finger towards the cardboard box. "You see all them books? The one who left them for Ray? He gone too."

He peeks out the front window. He can see Ray still standing on the sidewalk, staring down the block. He has already figured out that Ray is different, that something is not quite right. Him and his mother both stuck in the righteous purging of grief. One had history, the other had Kool-Aid, and from where Tony stood he couldn't see how either was doing them a bit of good.

He looks at the girl.

"Hey, girl. Look what I found."

Tony reaches into his pocket and pulls out the plastic bag full of white powder. He opens it up and pokes it with his finger.

"You know what this is?"

The girl stares down at it, then up at him. If she had to guess, she'd say sugar.

"It's medicinal is what it is," Tony says. "Like what the doctor give you when you got a cavity. Like Novocain. Rub it on your gums and the next thing you know, you can't feel a thing." He stands beside her and holds the bag open. "Go ahead and try it."

The girl stares back at him while he nods. She dips her finger inside the bag and rubs the powder onto her teeth.

"You see what I mean?"

A dry, metallic taste stretches up from her tongue, shoots through her nostrils, and clears a space for itself in the front of her brain.

"You see what I mean?"

All of a sudden she's dizzy. She sits down in the La-Z-Boy, struggling to keep her eyes open. Tony stands there, studying her face. After a moment he backs away from her slowly and sits down on the couch.

"I like you, girl. For real." He nods. "You just keep your head up. You'll be all right. You know why? Because you're cool. I could tell just as soon as I saw you, standing out on that porch."

He winks.

"That's why I want you to listen to me, okay? I'm gonna tell you a secret. And don't tell Ray I told you either. Because I love Ray's mama and all . . . she's like an auntie to me. But she also silly simple. You know what I mean?" He twirls his finger in the air near the side of his head. "Something not quite right. And if I were you I wouldn't drink any more of that woman's nasty Kool-Aid. You understand? Because I wouldn't . . ."

Tony shakes his head.

"Not even if you paid me."

8.

Raymond stands next to the curb, watching his mother's car pull into the driveway. When she opens the door and the light clicks on he can see the frantic look in her eyes, lips moving as she mutters to herself. She can't help him, he knows that. It's all she can do to keep herself upright, drag herself out of bed in the middle of the afternoon, open the door for her little flip babies, collect her parcel of dimes.

He helps his mother unload her grocery bags from the car and listens to her talk to herself. Blaming herself, trying to make sense of what happened. How could she have lost her son? How could things have possibly gone so wrong? What could she have done differently if only she had tried? She looks at Raymond, a quiet hysteria animating all her gestures: "Help me get these bags in the house. I've got work to do, I'm running out of time."

That is what is needed more than anything, he thinks. Time. So much history to sort through, struggling to make room for itself, scribbled in the margins of every page. The books he found in the back of his brother's closet are full of secrets, the private truths of a man talking to himself, whispering things that Raymond could scarcely imagine his brother saying out loud. Clearly Sam was standing on the precipice of a new understanding when he passed, and now there is no one to finish his thoughts but Raymond. He doesn't want to be interrupted. Not yet. He still needs time.

"Is that Tony sitting in my living room? Go tell that fool boy to come out here and help me with these bags—"

When Raymond walks back inside the house he takes one look at the girl sitting with her mouth hanging open and Tony shoving a plastic bag into the pocket of his jacket and knows that something is very wrong.

"What the fuck did you do?" he says, and Tony laughs. Tony laughs, even as Raymond pulls him up by the collar, pushes, and then hurls him towards the front door. Even in the midst of grief, Tony is still laughing.

"Remember what I told you, little girl. . . ."

A door slams. The girl can hear them scuffling out on the porch. She leans back in the La-Z-Boy and stares up at the ceiling, trying to negotiate the shifting rhythms of her own heartbeat. She is in the present, she is in a suburb of the south, and everything is quieter than before. There is no fist in the air, no promise of the Creative Unity Brigade. When she looks up she does not see the words from a book or her mother's hands or Aunt Ruby's face or the kids in the yard or the Rastafarians in a clinic waiting room. She doesn't see a needle or blue lights or even the little brick house across the street from Henry's Bar, where her uncle lives. When she looks up at the ceiling, she sees something even better.

A blank page.

And just as she is about to smile Raymond appears, hovering above the chair. She stares up at his pursed lips, dark eyes, eyebrow arched. He reaches around, takes her by the arm, and gently pulls her to her feet.

"Little girl? It's time for you to go home."

9.

The Flip Lady stands in her bright yellow kitchen, unpacking a bag of groceries. She takes out a large pot, fills it up with water from the sink, and sets it on the counter. She empties a canister of Kool-Aid and stirs. She adds a cup of sugar, watching the powder swirl through the purple liquid then disappear as it settles on the bottom. She thinks for a moment, then scoops out another cup.

"Little heathens." She chuckles. Just like Tony, always thinking she can't see past their smiles. But she watches everything from the kitchen window and she has seen it all. Nothing has changed. It's just like before: she always could tell the good from the bad.

"Bet y'all sleep good tonight," she mutters to herself. She doesn't do it for the money. No one has to thank her.

She smiles, thinks about all the little flip babies in this world. It doesn't last, nothing does. But for now they still come running, gather around her back porch, hold their hands out for the promise of something sweet.

And she gives it to them.

Henry

(1993)

You know what really bothered him? The disrespect. That was what Henry Moore found so intolerable. He'd had to go down to the courthouse that morning to pick up an eviction permit and happened to run into his brother Leon's lawyer in the parking garage. The encounter had so upset him that two hours later, sitting at the sidewalk table outside his bar, he was still thinking about it. The audacity of that lawyer, telling Henry what they were going to do, how things were already in motion, that they were already working on a new strategy to reopen Leon's case. Not asking, mind you, but telling him—as if Henry was just someone watching from the sidelines who didn't have anything to do with it. When everyone knew Henry was the guardian of Leon's legacy, the keeper of the flame. The one who'd been out there trying to hold Unity together until his big brother finally got out of prison.

Been like that for eight years now, ever since Leon got sent away on that trumped-up murder charge, police and prosecutor trying to make out like he was some vicious lunatic who went around killing innocent, unsuspecting police officers for no reason, save sheer hatred for the boys in blue. Leon was a dentist! A family man and respected member of his community, one who'd lived his whole life in the house where he was born. Everybody on the south side knew Leon, knew what kind of man he was, and therefore knew that he was not capable of committing such a stupid, senseless crime.

Outside of the south side too: for a while and for once it had seemed like people on the north side were actually paying attention and might just muster the courage to do the right thing. Before the trial there'd been an article in the newspaper, one that incorrectly described the south side as a "hopelessly blighted area" but which correctly detailed how his brother's efforts to advocate for his community had led to several unfortunate run-ins with the police. The article explained how a lot of the area's current problems could be traced to the former mayor's decision to build a highway that effectively cut the south side off from the rest of the city, how ever since the police seemed to be operating under a mandate to control and contain rather than protect and serve. They'd bulldozed the commercial strip, and in the years that followed there'd been a steep rise in complaints about civil rights violations, uses of excessive force, and unwarranted shootings. Leon formed his organization, Creative Unity Incorporated, as a means of coordinating efforts to resist such abuses, and thereafter had been subjected to what the article stated could only be characterized as a "systematic pattern of harassment."

While the article hadn't come out and called for Leon's acquittal, it made it clear that there was more than enough reason to doubt the prosecutor's claim that the shooting began with "a routine traffic stop." No, something more had gone on that night. An innocent man was being framed for murder, and for once it seemed like everyone understood that. For a few months there'd been a lot of protests and shouting and people promising to come together until justice was served, but in the end his brother was still convicted, sentenced to twenty-five years to life.

That was eight years ago. Eight years and, in the meantime, there was Henry, doing what he could to keep Unity together, to keep hope alive. Instead of moving to Chicago like he'd planned at the time of his brother's arrest, Henry had stayed, in part so he could look after Leon's wife, Trudy. Montgomery, Leon's first lawyer, got himself elected to the city council, and together he and Henry had worked to address high rates of unemployment on the south side. Henry had used the money he inherited from their father to buy the bar he was sitting in front of now, which gave him an opportunity to hire several men and women who, for various reasons, might have otherwise been considered unemployable. In that way he was investing in the community. Leon might not have approved of everything that went on in that bar, but the way Henry saw it, everyone deserved a drink now and then, a way to let off steam. Besides, these customers were paying the bills; without them he would not have been able to keep the community newsletter going, which, he was proud to say, still came out every month and on time.

Some of his brother's wilder ideas had had to be abandoned; nobody talked about sending delegations to Africa or setting up diplomatic relations in Cuba in exchange for medical training anymore. All of that was impractical, inflammatory and, truthfully? Most people never really understood what Leon had been trying to accomplish with all that Creative Unity Brigade talk, anyhow. Something about forging connections with other oppressed communities, working in solidarity through an understanding that what went on on the south side was not happening in isolation. All of which might have been true, but was also exhausting and confusing. Plus Henry knew for a fact that Leon's refusal to disassociate Unity from other, more radical groups had hurt him at the trial. Instead, under Henry's leadership, Unity had turned inward, redoubled its focus on what could be accomplished here, what could be done now. And if it was true that Unity had narrowed in ambition, it had also broadened in influence. Whenever people talked about giving back to the community, about their commitment to improving it as opposed to simply trying to get out, they were expressing core principles of Unity, whether they realized it or not.

How had Henry done that? By making sure there was a place for everyone in Unity, that whatever plans Unity had for the future would always include them. Under Henry's leadership Unity wasn't about excluding people, judging people, or alienating them with a lot of confusing ideas and outrageous demands. Unity was about compromise. It was about talking to people in a language they could not just admire but actually understand. He'd spent the past eight years making sure Unity had something to say to everybody, had decided that that was the key to maintaining a movement long-term. And he'd done these things not in support of his own vision but as a testament to his commitment to his brother's.

All he asked for in return was a little respect. Instead of telling Henry what was going to happen, that lawyer should have been consulting Henry on strategy, asking Henry's permission before he even thought about making a next move. After all Henry had done over the past eight years, it was the least he deserved.

"Everything all right?"

Henry looked up and saw Paulie Sparks, one of his employees, standing over him. He was holding a bag from the Byrdie's Burgers across the street, which contained Henry's lunch. He set it down on the table.

Henry shook his head. "You know, back in my daddy's day, people dealt with white folks the same as if you were still in the jungle and surrounded by a bunch of wild animals. Do not feed or molest. Keep your head down, try not to make eye contact, and keep your dealings with them to a minimum. I know nowadays a lot of people think they did that out of fear, but it wasn't that, or not just that. It was strategy."

He looked at Paulie.

"See? My daddy had a family to think about, a lot of people depending on him. And because those people were his primary concern, he had to always be thinking about how they would be affected by his actions, the choices he made. Whenever he was tempted to get into some fight, he had to remember what it was he was actually fighting for. Because those people who were depending on him didn't need him flying off the handle, getting himself killed trying to prove a point. They needed him to stay alive, to be smart enough to figure out what he had to do to survive so that he could help them survive too."

Paulie stared.

"Now things change, I realize things have changed," Henry said. "Keeping your head down is not always appropriate to the situation. If anyone understands that, it's me. Take my brother, for example. They built that highway, tore up the neighborhood. My brother knew someone had to do something. Someone had to stand up, fight for this community. And Leon did that knowing full well what the consequences might be. Understood the situation, what was at stake. He figured it was worth the risk."

"Your brother is a hero," Paulie said.

"Damn right, he's a hero," Henry said. "But he's been sitting in jail for, what, eight years now? And during that time he's had Black lawyers and he's had white lawyers. Used to have Montgomery working on his case until he decided to run for office. Leon has got that white lawyer now and . . . I don't know. The man has been working with us for seven years without charging no fee. And he acts like he's doing it out of the kindness of his heart, but maybe you get what you pay for. Sometimes I'll listen to him talk, going on and on about injustice and the system, and I'll think, *That's all well and good but how is it a strategy?* Because it seems to me that if he's representing my brother he ought to have but one simple ambition in life, and that is to get Leon out of jail."

Henry shook his head. "One time he actually says to me, 'Your brother is a tragic symbol of the systematic racism entrenched within the Prison Industrial Complex.' But, see, he's not a symbol. Not to me. He's my brother."

"Some people might say we not the ones responsible for making him a symbol," Paulie said. "Some people might say that's why we can't forget."

"Yeah? Maybe." Henry frowned. "Anyhow, I got feelings about it. Because it seems to me you can't win no fight if you don't know what you're fighting for. And in this particular situation, sometimes I wonder if my daddy wasn't right about the feeding and molesting. Like maybe it's long past time to accept that all the protests and petitions and trying to call folks out by their names has got a kind of counterweight to it. I mean, think about it, everybody in this city with half a brain already knows Leon didn't go out that night trying to kill anybody, knows he was just trying to defend himself. And if they already know, what's the point in talking about it? Maybe instead of reminding people of things they already know, we ought to be trying to make them forget. Stop dredging up the past and stirring up a lot of bad feelings, just let everybody put it behind them. Stop trying to turn my brother into a symbol, making him so conspicuous. See if we can't slip him out the back door that way."

Paulie blinked.

"Like I said, I got feelings about it," Henry said.

"Well, of course you do," Paulie said. "That's just normal. He's your brother, so of course it's gonna look different to you than it does to everybody else."

"Yeah?" Henry nodded. "What do you think?"

"Me?"

"Yeah, you. You're the one standing there. Who else would I be talking to?"

"I don't know," Paulie said. "I mean about the lawyer. You say he's stuck with you for seven years and not getting paid for it? That's a long time. Plus he one of them, right? I mean, according to your daddy's logic, he's one of the wild animals. Seem like maybe he might know a way to deal with them that's different from how you might see it."

"If he knows how to deal with it, then why is my brother still in jail?"

Paulie thought for a moment. "I don't know," he said.

Henry nodded. "Well, thanks for that. Very insightful. Very helpful."

"Sure thing," Paulie said. He started to walk back inside but then stopped.

"Maybe you should talk to Marcus."

"Marcus?" Henry was surprised to hear the name of another one of his employees.

"He's the one who's been talking to that lawyer." Paulie shrugged. "Went to see him just last week. Said Leon asked him to deliver a package for him the last time you sent him out there."

Henry nodded. That was another thing he'd been doing for the past eight years, making sure someone went to check up on Leon twice a month. When he couldn't do it himself he sent one of the young men who worked for him. For the past nine months, this person had been Marcus. But this was the first time he'd heard anything about a package.

"Tell Marcus to come to my office. Tell him I need to speak to him. Tell him I said now."

He picked up his sandwich and followed Paulie back inside. They walked past the row of red booths by the front window, where a woman was busy wiping down tables. When they reached the bar, Paulie turned left, headed for the kitchen, while Henry kept straight, heading towards his office. He unlocked the door, turned on the lights, and stepped inside.

He sat down at his desk. While he waited, he finished his sandwich and wondered why Leon would send Marcus to talk to his lawyer, why Marcus hadn't said anything about it. He figured it must have had something to do with this new strategy the lawyer had told him about which, so far as he could tell, wasn't new and wasn't even a strategy, properly speaking. Even before their brief encounter in the parking lot that morning, Henry had never really liked that lawyer, never trusted his intentions. He'd tried to tell Leon that the last time he went to see him. But Leon wouldn't listen; he'd been in a bad mood that day, was agitated for some reason and kept asking the same question over and over.

Have you been dealing drugs out of the bar?

This had irritated Henry. One, because of course it wasn't true and two, because it wasn't what they were talking about.

They were talking about something else.

There was a knock on the door.

"You wanted to see me?"

Henry looked up as Marcus stuck his head inside the doorway. His upper lip was swollen and there was a nasty cut on his left cheek.

"What the heck happened to you?"

Marcus shut the door. He lumbered inside, a big hulking kid with warm brown eyes, mumbling to himself as he made his way across the floor.

"Don't worry about it," he said.

"Don't worry about it? What do you mean, 'Don't worry about it'?" Henry shook his head. "You work for me, remember? That means everything you do reflects back on me and this bar. If you've been out in the street, running around getting in fights again, I need to know."

Marcus sucked his teeth. He sank down in the seat across from Henry's desk, legs splayed in front of him. He was mumbling again, and maybe it was the swollen lip, but Henry couldn't make out what he was saying.

"What? What's that you said? Speak up, boy." All he heard was something about a cousin.

"You met her," Marcus said. "A couple of weeks ago, the one who came in with Sean."

"Sean?"

"One who got hit in the head with the bottle."

Henry frowned as he recalled the night Marcus was referring to. Sean Thompson, Montgomery's personal driver, had come with some sloppy girl Henry had never met before. From what Paulie told him, they'd started getting loud almost as soon as they walked through the door. Henry didn't know about the situation until it was clear they were disturbing his other customers. He'd put them both out.

"What about her?"

Marcus shook his head, still mumbling. "Just crazy is all."

"What is crazy? Sean is crazy? Your cousin is crazy?"

"Yes. I mean I guess so. . . . I mean no." Marcus shifted in his seat. "Not like that. It's the condition. She had the condition."

"The condition?"

"Leon told me about it. One time when you sent me up there to check up on him. Like, when you in a bad situation and start to tell yourself you like it. Because if you like it then you're the one who's in control. When really it's just being scared."

Henry nodded. "Stockholm syndrome."

"That's right," Marcus said. "That's what Leon called it. My cousin's scared to leave him so she starts telling herself it's something else. Make like she wants to be there, then after a while, starts to believe it's true."

"What's any of that got to do with you fighting in the street?"

"I don't know," Marcus said. He shifted in his seat again. "Nothing, maybe. Maybe it just means I don't got it."

Henry shook his head. This was what he had to deal with. And it was sad because he liked Marcus, knew how smart he was, how much potential the boy had. There was a reason Marcus was the one Henry sent to check up on Leon. He knew how much his brother liked Marcus too.

If only the boy could learn to control his temper.

"Stockholm syndrome, huh? And you don't have it? That's what you're telling me? Well, good for you, Marcus Johnson. You know what you do have? A job. A chance to do something constructive with your life. But the only way you are going to keep that chance is if you stop getting in fights. You don't approve of your cousin's relationship with Sean? Okay. I get that. But she's a grown woman, is she not? Means you've got to respect her choices, even if you don't understand them. Unless there's something I'm not getting here. Something you're not telling me. Like if she wants to leave him and he won't let her do that—"

"I told you. She said she was happy with him. He made her drop out of school."

"Well, if she's happy, then how is fighting in the street going to help?" Henry said. "You can't solve every problem with your fists, son. Got to be smarter than that. Keep doing like you do, you'll just wind up in jail or worse. And then what? How are you going to help your cousin then? How are you going to help anybody if you stuck in jail?"

Marcus glared at him. "That why you wanted to talk to me? You worried about me fighting with Sean?"

"Actually, no." Henry sighed. "Paulie tells me you've been to see Leon's lawyer. That you delivered some kind of package to him."

"That's right."

"Mind telling me what was in it?"

Marcus shifted in his seat. He shrugged. "Notes."

"Notes?"

"Transcripts of some interviews Leon's been doing . . . Don't want nobody to know he doing it until it's finished. But he's writing a book."

"A book?"

"Yeah. Says he's come to understand a lot of things since going to that prison. Thinks it's about time people really knew what's going on in there. Says if they don't know what's going on in there, they won't ever really understand what's going on out here. Says people need to understand what they are fighting for."

"What are you talking about?" Henry squinted. "Are you talking about an exposé, Marcus? Are you saying that my brother wants to write an exposé of the prison *he's still stuck in?*"

"Not wants to." Marcus shook his head. "He's already doing it. Lawyer thinks it's a good idea. Thinks maybe if we get a book out, might get people talking about Leon again, put some pressure on the DA's office to reopen Leon's case, try to get the conviction overturned."

"Overturned? Because of a book?" Henry could feel his heart beating faster in his chest. "Boy, that's not how shit works. Nothing has ever been overturned by a book. All y'all doing is making my brother more of a target than he already is. Make it so he never gets out."

Marcus shrugged. "Leon said not much different between being in and the kind of out you talking about anyway. He says that the truth is the way out."

"That right?" Henry said. He could feel his left eye starting to twitch. "Tell me something Marcus. When you sitting there, listening to him talk about truth and being free, does it ever occur to you that my brother has been locked up *for eight years?* Does it occur to you that maybe all this talk about not needing to get out might have something to do with him starting to think he never will? Has it ever occurred to you that maybe my brother is traumatized?"

"Yeah, we talked about that too," Marcus said. "About being traumatized."

Henry slammed his fist on his desk. "Well, I'm not letting you do it, you hear me? There's not gonna be no book. I'll fire that lawyer myself before I let Leon do something like that."

Marcus shrugged. "Well, Leon's a grown man, right? Like my cousin. He can do what he wants and you don't have to like it but—"

"Don't play with me, boy! This is not a joke. I want my brother out! You hear me, Marcus?"

He took a deep breath and tried to calm down. "You all really are crazy, aren't you? And you know something? I bet deep down my brother knows it." He shook his head. "No wonder Leon was so upset the last time I went to see him."

"No," Marcus said. "That's not why Leon's upset. He's upset because somebody told him you were dealing drugs out of the bar."

"What?" Henry blinked. "You know that's not true."

"I'm not the one who said it. Somebody else must have told him about it. But don't worry, I got it straightened out. I told him it was Sean."

"Sean?"

"Told Leon how Sean's been supplying Montgomery with cocaine and in exchange Montgomery has been letting him drive his car. Told him how ever since that started, Sean been walking around, acting like he can do whatever he wants on account of he's on Montgomery's payroll. I told Leon that whoever said you were the one dealing drugs must have got confused on account of the fact that Montgomery hangs out in the bar so much and whenever he and Sean want some privacy, you let them use your office."

Henry cocked his head. "Why would you tell my brother that?"

"Because it's the truth," Marcus said. "It's not like it's a secret. Sean brags about it all the time, how he know all about Montgomery's business. Even brags about knowing where Montgomery hides his stash. Got an old freezer in the back of his garage, keep all kinds of drugs and money locked inside it. Montgomery says it's the safest place because it's the last place anybody would think to look. Plus his wife never goes back there. Seems like the only person Montgomery is worried about knowing his business is his wife."

"Stop talking. You hear me? You shouldn't be talking about things you don't know nothing about."

"Thought you'd be happy, me going to the trouble to let Leon know that you aren't the problem."

Henry squinted. "Has it occurred to you that maybe you are the problem?"

"Yes," Marcus said. "It has."

Henry shook his head. "What is this, Marcus? Is this about your cousin? I mean, you got some kind of issue with Sean and now you're trying to drag my brother into it, drag Montgomery into it? You upset because of your cousin, that's a personal problem and that's how you need to keep it. Personal. Trust me, all you're doing now is causing more problems. How is any of this going to help your cousin?"

"It's not," Marcus said. He stood up. "Anyhow, she dead now."

"What?" Henry thought about all the mumbling when Marcus first walked into the office. "Is that what you were trying to tell me?"

He looked at Marcus. He started to ask if Sean had actually killed his cousin but realized they would probably be having a very different conversation if he had. Things would have been more straightforward.

"I didn't know. I mean, I didn't hear you. You didn't articulate yourself. You have to articulate yourself more clearly."

"I articulate myself just fine," Marcus said. He started walking towards the door. "Is that all? You don't want me fighting with Sean? You don't want me helping Leon with his book?"

"Wait a minute, now," Henry called after him. "Marcus? Listen to me now. I'm going to talk to Montgomery, tell him he needs to do something about Sean. You and me, we can find a way to make this right. But you got to stop what you're doing. Hear me? You got a problem, you come to me, let me help you. Don't drag Montgomery's name into it. Because when you attack Montgomery, you are attacking the entire community. He is our representative. No one wants to hear these kinds of accusations. No good will come of it. You hear me, Marcus?"

"I hear you," Marcus said.

Henry sighed. "And don't talk about stuff like that with my brother anymore. All you're doing is upsetting him, getting him agitated. What do you expect my brother to do for you anyhow, when he's stuck in jail? He can't help you, son. He's not even here."

"No." Marcus frowned. "He's not."

He shut the door behind him.

Bitch:
An Etymology
of Family Values

(1994)

1.

Fine day at the top of Cobb Hill. The sun was shining, the breeze was blowing, and the ladies of the executive planning committee were out on Mrs. Montgomery's patio discussing entertainment ideas for the end of the month's fundraiser and fashion show. In the past they'd always gone with an evening of classic jazz, but this year some members wanted to try something different, something that might resonate with today's youth. What about that rap person one of them had heard their kids talking about? Freshie Fresh? Pearlie Pearl? Melle Mel.

And in between brainstorming they were laughing and chatting and snacking on chips and homemade salsa prepared by Porsche, the Montgomerys' maid. Sipping glasses of chilled Zinfandel, flicking ash in the silver ashtray. Staring out at the view of the valley while Marvin Gaye crooned from the living room speakers: *Got to give it up.* The wine was flowing, the wind chimes were swaying. The telephone was ringing, and Porsche had already left for the day.

"Excuse me," Mrs. Montgomery said as she pushed back her chair. She walked across the patio, high heels clicking on the wooden floorboards, bangles on her wrist sparkling as she pulled back the patio door. She stepped onto the white tiles of the living room, strode past the entertainment center and the red leather sofa. She reached for the princess phone on the marble-countered bar.

"Hello?" Mrs. Montgomery said.

"Ma'am?" a woman's voice called back softly. "He don't love you no more."

"What?"

"Your husband. The councilman," the voice said—a shy country accent with a shrill, nervous tone. "He lied to me just like he's been lying to you."

"Who is this?"

"He's done a lot of dirt since he got elected. And now he's going down."

Mrs. Montgomery shook her head. "Listen, I don't know how you got this number—"

"How you think I got it? He gave it to me."

Mrs. Montgomery gritted her teeth. She glanced back at the women on her patio, still smiling and nodding on the other side of the glass. She lowered her head and pivoted around so that she was facing the kitchen door.

"Bitch, are you deaf?" she said. "I just told you I don't care how you got this number. This is *my* house, you understand?"

"Who you calling bitch?" the voice said.

"You do not call *my* house," Mrs. Montgomery said. "I will not be harassed by some prostitute. You hear me, you whore?"

"I'm just trying to warn you is all—"

"Then let me return the favor," Mrs. Montgomery said. "You call my house again and I promise you'll regret it. Who the hell do you think you are?"

"I'm the bitch who's fucking him," the voice said.

For the next few minutes Mrs. Montgomery stood alone in the living room clutching the princess phone to her ear. As if she hadn't heard the click of the receiver and didn't realize her other party was gone. She stared blankly at the patio where her guests were still laughing—hoisting salsa onto blue corn chips, lighting another Kool—as if in a state of shock. Yet even in her initial disorientation, one thought was perfectly clear: her husband was going to pay.

She could make him pay. No one knew the man's secrets better than she did, knew what a weak man he was and in truth had always been. Even back in his activist days, when they were not husband and wife, but friends and allies committed to a common cause. Back when he was still a civil rights attorney who spent his free time handing out flyers in support of Creative Unity. Back when she could still stand to listen when he came home in the middle of the night, weeping as he confessed the twin addictions he claimed had plagued him since puberty.

"Hooch and cooch." He'd shake his head bitterly, as if it were the name of a disease. There'd been a time when the man had so much charisma he could charm her pants off even as he sat there swearing he couldn't help himself.

A whole lot had changed since then. They'd gone from sleeping on a used mattress in a studio apartment to living in a big house on Cobb Hill. They'd gone from standing in the rain on picket lines to shaking hands with city leaders and attending meetings at City Hall. First Reagan then Bush and now Clinton had moved into the White House, and while a lot of their former allies had given up or been forced underground, they drove through town in Mercedes convertibles and shopped for designer clothes. Yet even in this, Mrs. Montgomery thought, they were only doing what was expected of them.

The people wanted to see their leaders in positions of power and living well; it gave them something to aspire to.

Yes, a whole lot had changed. And yet, in other ways, it was just like always. The Montgomerys were still out on the frontlines, still fighting the good fight. Her husband still needed someone to clean him up every now and then.

"Delia?"

She looked up and saw one of the ladies slide back the patio door.

"Are you all right?"

Mrs. Montgomery studied the other woman's face. Had any of her guests overheard that distasteful outburst on the phone? She'd been careful to whisper, but as she replayed the conversation in her mind it came back to her not simply as undignified, but loud.

"I'm fine," Mrs. Montgomery said and hung up the phone. She straightened her back, took a deep breath, and returned to the patio. Smiling and waving, moving quickly across the floor, heels clicking in time to the unpleasant memory of her own voice resonating in her head:

Bitch bitch bitch bitch bitch . . .

2.

Down in the valley, in a small apartment near the edge of the interstate, Bechibaya Jones gripped a handle and pushed, then stuck her head through the bedroom door.

"Who you talking to in there, Millicent Jones?"

For one hot moment Millie mistook her grandmother for an ass whooping and jumped. "Nothing I mean nobody I mean why?"

Bechibaya squinted. Millie was wearing a red tank top and a

bright yellow miniskirt hiked halfway up her thigh, legs sprawled out in front of her and cotton balls wedged between her still-wet toes. She looked guilty.

"You're not making long-distance calls on my telephone again are you, Millie? What did I tell you about that?"

"I wasn't," Millie said.

The old woman looked at her granddaughter and sighed. "Twenty-four going on twelve," she said. Then she shook her head and backed out the way she came.

Millie waited until her grandmother shut the door. She looked down at the fuchsia polish on her still-wet toes and thought, *Why, that flat-chested no-ass-having stuck-up bitch just called me a fucking* prostitute.

Millie was not a prostitute. She had men friends and they helped her out from time to time, but that was just what men friends do. What was wrong with that?

Isn't that just normal? she wished she'd said. *Doesn't your husband help you out?* If she was a prostitute, do you think she would still be working three shifts a week at Henry's Bar just to cover the rent on some crappy apartment she shared with her grandmother? You could be damn sure she would not.

Millie's eyes scanned the small room as if she still expected that ass whooping to come jumping out of her closet or stretch a hand out from under her bed and grab her by her ankles. Montgomery had warned her what he would do if she ever got too stupid or pushed him too far. The man had a smooth smile, clean, clipped nails, and she'd known him for a long time. Still, she did not doubt for a second that he was telling her the truth. Just like she knew that were the situation reversed—if he was the one being harassed by the police and told that the only way to help himself was to testify against her—the man would not have hesitated to give her up. And so the only reason she had hesitated was that she was trying to wrap her mind around what the situation actually was.

"Graft, money laundering, peddling of influence, trafficking in illegal substances—"

All of which was no doubt a shame. Millie just didn't see what any of it had to do with her.

"I don't know anything about any of that," she'd told the police. "The councilman and I, we're just friends, not even. Just know some of the same people is all. But he doesn't talk about his business with me."

Then they'd asked her about the freezer in the councilman's garage. The truth was she did know about that; she'd overheard Montgomery say something about it to Henry one night when they were hanging out at the bar. The only reason it had stuck in her mind was because it seemed like such a stupid place to keep money.

"That's the whole point," Montgomery said when she asked him about it later. Then gave her a cold look as if disgusted by her lack of understanding as to what made something a good place to hide.

"Make no mistake," the police had told her. "You will be charged as an accessory after the fact. Do this, or you will go to jail."

Yet somehow, in the midst of all that drama, there she was trying to help a sister out, give the wife a heads up when she didn't have to do that. She'd already called twice that afternoon, then hung up when the maid answered the phone. She wanted to speak to the wife woman-to-woman; after five years you'd think she had the right. She could have been the next Mrs. Montgomery for all that bitch knew, *stepmama to your child, so show some motherfucking respect.* Could have been. At least that's what she thought at first. But she was only nineteen when she started dating Montgomery. Now she was twenty-four.

Millie looked around until her eyes settled on the posters tacked on her walls and could feel herself start to calm down. Wedged between Tupac, Prince, and Jodeci were pictures of women in bikinis, sunning themselves on the beaches of Ipanema, parading barefoot through the streets of Salvador, Brazil. Pictures of places that, if she stared at them long enough, she started to forget she'd never been. Her father's mother was Brazilian by way of New Orleans, and Millie had decided that that explained a lot of things. The fucked-up spelling of Bechibaya's first name, the swivel in Millie's own hips. The feeling Millie often had like she didn't know what she was doing here and had just been plopped down in a world where she didn't quite belong. It wasn't until she moved in with Bechibaya and had a look through the old photo albums that she started to piece together a way to make sense of it: where that swivel came from, why it seemed to have so much power. It was the swivel that had gotten her the job at Henry's, what had first attracted Montgomery to her side. But it was also what made her mama bar the door all those years ago, what she meant when she looked down at Millie and said, "I love you, girl, but you can't come back here."

Millie was sixteen, standing on the front porch with her face all busted up and those ugly green stitches hanging off her lower lip. When she looked up she could see her stepfather standing in the shadows of the hallway, shaking his head and staring down at the floor.

"Can't speak?" Millie said, her stepfather having been the first one to point it out. The swivel: said he could hear it calling to him all through the house, said he could smell it in his sleep. And maybe if Millie had thought to tell her mother about that before she ran away, a lot of things would have been different. But as it was she'd been gone for almost a year.

"I love you, Millie, but I just can't cope with it no more. . . ."

That was when Millie looked down and realized her mother's belly was sticking out to here. She stared at her mother's stomach for a moment, then walked away laughing—because the doctor had already told her it was something she would never have.

Which was fine with Montgomery because he didn't "believe" in condoms anyway—he said his penis needed to breathe. Used to talk all kinds of trifling nonsense when they first started dating and Millie used to just laugh right along with him, not because she was stupid or crazy, whatever else he might have thought. Maybe she laughed because she was a fucking human being and it didn't do no good to cry. But it had to come out some kind of way. So sometimes that was what she was laughing at: the no good that crying did.

Well, a whole lot had changed since then. She didn't have to laugh anymore if she didn't feel like it. Because she was only nineteen when she first started dating him. Now she was almost thirty.

Fuck all y'all quite frankly and as a matter of fact, Millie thought. She pulled the cotton balls out of her toes, slipped into a pair of heels, and walked into the living room where Bechibaya sat slumped in the easy chair watching the TV news. When Millie passed by, the woman turned her head and gave her granddaughter a look that was startled and sleepy and old.

"Millie? You all right?"

"I'm going out," Millie said and stomped out the front door.

3.

". . . Who the hell do you think you are?"

Rosalie Rousson stood hunched in the doorway in a tan suit she'd borrowed from her mother, asking herself the exact same thing. Behind her back she could hear the tinkling of ice in hoisted glasses, the laughing of the ladies on the patio. They were all so successful, so secure in their seamless circle while she was still so unsure of her place. They were all slightly older than she was, but still. Even if she compared herself to where they were seven or eight years ago, she knew she was off to a late start. She had to step quickly if she wanted to catch up, had to stay focused, smile, and stay sharp. She stood in the doorway and shifted her weight from right to left.

Rosalie peered inside the living room, stared at the clenched grip of Delia's hand on the telephone's receiver, and listened to the sharp sound of angry curses insufficiently drowned out by the music still playing on the turntable. Why did Rosalie so often find herself lurking in corners where she clearly did not belong? That was not her intention at all. Yet this was in fact the second awkward conversation she had been subjected to that day, having senselessly stumbled within earshot of the few choice words her hostess had expressed to Porsche the maid on her way out the kitchen door. Rosalie had no idea who Delia Montgomery was yelling at now, but thankfully it wasn't her.

At least not yet. Rosalie pressed her shoulder against the door and shifted her weight from left to right. She wondered if it was possible to simply back out the way she came. But she'd stood up from the table with the expressed purpose of using the bathroom, and to deviate from that course of action now would require some sort of explanation. It seemed impossible to simply return to her seat without someone asking her why.

Why, Rosalie, go to the trouble of making such a spectacle of yourself by crossing the patio only to abruptly stop once you've reached the door?

For a moment she felt trapped where she was, hopelessly burdened by the desire to make a good impression and therefore not do anything Delia or the other ladies might consider odd or otherwise disruptive to the status quo. The result was disorientation: it made her feel light-headed somehow, although she was not certain if this was simply an effect of the throbbing of her foot, wedged as it was in a low pump a half size too small. She knew before she left her apartment that afternoon—as she was kissing her daughter on the cheek, promising to be home within the hour—that there was a blister on her left big toe, and she now suspected it had burst and was bleeding.

She lifted her left shoe off the wood planks of the patio and stepped onto the living room floor.

"Delia? Are you all right?"

Delia wheeled around, and for one hideous moment, Rosalie saw herself as surely her hostess saw her: the borrowed and the bloodied, the recently divorced. The one who left Cobb Hill twelve years ago with a full scholarship to Bryn Mawr and now had nothing to show for herself but an entry-level job at the local paper where she proofread and poured coffee because at least it was a foot in the door.

"I'm fine," Delia said and hung up the phone. She brushed past Rosalie as she pushed her way outside.

Rosalie stood there for a moment and stared at the empty room. The record stopped and she watched the needle slide across the turntable, clicking as it came to a rest in its holder. The last time she'd been to the Montgomery's house it was a cocktail party; she'd been standing by an hors d'oeuvres table when she felt something slide across her backside. She didn't even realize it was Mr. Montgomery's hand until after she'd jerked around and spilled her wine across the front of the man's shirt. She told her mother about it when she got home, and after that they had never discussed it again. Her mother had assured her there was nothing to discuss. Not if she wanted to get ahead in this town, not if she wanted some semblance of a career. Only now she wondered, did Delia know about that hand? Hold Rosalie responsible for it, somehow?

She tried not to think about that, tried to focus on her foot. She took a deep breath, straightened her back, and hobbled across the tiles until she reached the guest bathroom, where everything was immaculate and white.

Rosalie stood in front of the sink. She felt the safety pin affixed to the elastic waistband of her skirt poking her in the side as she leaned forward and carefully removed her pumps, then stared at the dark smears of blood spread across the bottom seams of her panty hose.

She stood back up and reached under her skirt, securing the tight waistband of her support hose with the tips of her fingers and pulling the thick elastic down across her hips and thighs. The thin synthetic material unfurled over her calves, feet, and finally, her toes.

She held the hose out in front of her like a shed skin fluttering in the light pouring from the open window above the sink. Through it, she could hear the murmured conversation of the ladies outside: "Delia, dear, are you all right? Who was that on the phone?"

"Nothing, I mean no one . . . just a wrong number—"

To them Rosalie had sacrificed her day of compensation, the one day of the week when she did not work, meant to make up for the heavy rotation of daycare and babysitters that had come to encompass her daughter's life since the divorce. She had promised she would only be gone for an hour and had already sat on that patio for almost three.

She looked down at her foot, the congealing blood merging with chipped red polish on her left big toe. She knew her mother was right, that she needed these women, needed their connections, needed to network if she wanted to have some semblance of a career. But still.

Fucking bitches, she thought to herself. A thought that quickly morphed into *You, bitch, you*. That was the last thing she remembered her husband saying to her on the day their divorce was finalized, a whispered promise breathed into her ear on his way out the door: *Lying bitch. You, bitch, you. Good luck with your new life. Good luck with your plans.*

She rolled the stockings into a ball and stuffed them in her purse. She gripped the edge of the sink, shut her eyes, and forced her naked foot back into the shoe. The pain was excruciating, but when she looked up and saw her own distorted grimace shining back at her in the mirror there was sudden humor in it. So she laughed.

She had a daughter to support and stared at her face in the mirror until her features managed to smooth back down into a semblance of calm. She had a daughter to support and went through the whole thing of flushing the toilet, then running the water in the sink as if she were washing her hands. She had a daughter to support and just in case they were listening they could rest assured not a thing was amiss. And she was so grateful to have been asked to join the committee, to be invited back to that smooth circle of ladies who once had been her peers. She would force herself to fit.

4.

"Delia, dear, are you all right? Who was that on the phone?"

Delia looked up and this is what she saw: skin like cooked cream, hazel eyes, straight nose, narrow lips puckered around the rim of a wineglass. The oral surgeon educated at Howard, the tooth puller, the applier of anesthesia, the recently retired. Hair thick and coarse but straight, pulled back into a rust-and-salt-colored bun. Once the judge's beautiful wife, now the judge's generous widow. Crucial supporter of her husband's campaign.

"Nothing, I mean no one," Delia said. She poured herself a glass of wine. "Just a wrong number."

"Really?" the widow said. "I could have sworn I heard you arguing with someone in there. For a moment you sounded upset. . . ."

"Not at all," Delia said.

The widow sipped her wine and looked out towards the sunset, her shadowy smile casting a wide net towards the sky.

Lying bitch, the widow thought. *Stupid woman, silly, simple shrew.* Too dumb to realize that all she would ever have to hide behind was her husband's last name. She had married a Montgomery, and instead of lifting the man up she had made him miserable, and everyone knew that was why he carried on with such audacity.

The widow smiled. Oh, they all went back a long time. Back to when Ellory Montgomery was still an attorney working in the public defender's office and Delia Montgomery was still just Delia Song. The judge's wife was ten years older than they were, but back then all that made her was a woman.

Once the judge's beautiful wife: wooed and won while still in college, the judge already well established, well past middle age. A distinguished salt-and-pepper man with strong hands, an intelligent forehead, and piercing brown eyes rimmed with integrity.

Like tears: *Are we somehow responsible?* Of strength: *What man simply sits idly by while mere children languish in jails?* And faultless vision: how clearly he had foreseen the consequences of Birmingham, all those years ago. What the students lacked was not courage but discipline, the judge told her. Born of anger, an entire generation of nihilistic, undisciplined youth were being bred on false promises and unrealistic expectations. The patience of strategy, that was how our people had survived. It was why he invited the young lawyer Montgomery over for drinks.

The widow still remembered the first time she saw Ellory Montgomery standing speechless in her parlor, the startled look on his face when she entered the room. The judge laughed. *So it is when an old man has a young and beautiful wife*, then he asked about the dreadful condition at the jailhouse; how the protesters were holding up, what there was to be done. Ellory smiled and clasped the widow's hand. When he explained that the situation required certain sacrifice, there was no doubting his commitment and the sincerity of his vision.

But sometimes sincerity was not the issue, the judge insisted. It was why he was writing his book. Part memoir, part family history and testimonial to all his ancestors had accomplished, not despite Negroness, the judge corrected, but because of. Ellory leaned forward and kissed the widow's hand. *Nihilism*, the judge said, and offered Ellory another drink. The result of a lack of history. He said he understood the frustration, even sympathized. But not the recklessness.

All ancient history now, long past rumors spun in secret and the

lie of proximity. Was it really possible that their affair had lasted for
less than a year? Yet the feel of that first glance, its potential to topple
everything, had been swirling in the widow's heart like butterflies for
years. Even now she could feel it, the shock of skin against skin, the
first time Ellory touched her reverberating like a warm tingle between
her thighs. But she would not leave the judge. Impossible, unthink-
able; the nihilism of it went against her very nature. And so eventually, Ellory had married a Song.

That one there: Delia, who had never lost that tiresome silliness
about her; it turned out to have nothing to do with age. It was simply
who she was, and no amount of camouflage would ever cover it, not
money, not even time.

The widow looked across the patio and, almost as if to confirm it,
saw shy, sad Rosalie Rousson skulking back to her corner of the table.
The poor girl had made a bad marriage and was paying her penance.
Still, there was no denying who she was. A Rousson: granddaughter
of Eugene, daughter of Hugo. The widow had no doubt that one day
Rosalie would rise, phoenix-like, to the occasion of her given name.

The widow stared down at her hands on the table. One day they
had started to wrinkle, skin still soft but parched somehow, and what a
strange sensation that had been. But she would always be a handsome
woman. Ellory could still be hers with a snap of her fingers, a simple
silent please.

She could feel Delia's nervous eyes upon her, and she smiled. *Perhaps the others don't remember where you came from, but I do. I am twice
the woman you ever were, Delia Song, and always will be. Your husband
is heartbroken, for he has never fully recovered from loving me. And one
day you will understand it, that it was not the carrying on so much as the
audacity that confirmed it: misery.*

The widow sipped her wine. *Delia Song*. That was her given name
and, in truth, always would be. Maybe the others had forgotten, but

not her. *Might have married a Montgomery, but still*, the widow thought. *Still just a Song.*

5.

The next time people saw Councilman Montgomery was on the eve-ning news. Featured artist in a black-and-white video so grainy and dark they might not have recognized him were it not for his name superimposed across the bottom of the screen. Just a slumped shadow removing his jacket, tossing his keys on the dresser, sitting on the edge of the bed in a motel room while a woman in a red tank top and short yellow skirt buzzed around in front of him. He barely had time to light the pipe when the door swung open and the police burst in, guns drawn and inexplicably dressed in riot gear.

After that: the mad scramble across the bed, the wild scuffle of feet diving towards the bathroom door, much of it obscured by the woman standing in front of the camera, whooping and hollering and flailing her arms in an effort to get out of the way.

But as far as the students of Ben Franklin Elementary were con-cerned, the best part came after the shouting and tumult was over, after everything had calmed down and he was seated on the edge of the bed with his hands cuffed behind his back. He looked down at the floor, shook his head, then rolled his eyes up to the ceiling as if he still didn't realize he was being watched.

"I don't believe it," they heard him say. "Bitch set me up—"

And everybody laughed.

Of course everybody laughed. How could you not laugh when it was such a good line, the kind of line that just felt good to say, was purging somehow. There were always so many good opportunities to

purge, and somehow, such a need. The first time they heard it repeated was during PE class the next morning. A whole group of them
were playing dodgeball when Tamika Montgomery came running
across the field, looking weepy and distracted and fifteen minutes late.
Someone threw her the ball and she caught it, took two steps forward,
and tripped over those big feet of hers. The ball skidded from her
hands, hit the pavement, and bounced with a loud whomp! Right
into Latonya Kendrick's stomach.

The impact knocked the wind out of Latonya, and for a moment
she just stood there hunched over. Everybody stopped what they were
doing, even the wind got quiet as if the whole world were waiting to
see how Latonya would react, how much the reverberations hurt, if
she was mad about it or not. Then suddenly she straightened up and
pointed at Tamika.

"I don't believe it," Latonya said. "Bitch set me up!"

Everyone laughed because in truth it was hysterical; even Tamika
laughed, although maybe she was just relieved that Latonya was not
threatening to kick her ass, which, knowing Latonya, she might just
as easily have done. But it was too good a line, too easy a setup for
even Latonya to squander that day. By lunchtime everybody had heard
about it and they were all saying it. It seemed like anything anybody
did that remotely resembled betrayal was just another opportunity for
a setup, police bursting in, guns drawn.

After a few weeks people stopped calling each other bitches on
a daily basis; it just kind of got played out. They got tired of hearing
it all the time, and so they moved on to other things. In the year
that followed it was only used sparingly, its meaning depending on
the speaker or circumstance. By the time the newspaper published
its five-part exposé of government corruption, by the time Councilman Montgomery was sent to prison and Mrs. Montgomery filed for
divorce, they'd all heard it hissed in absolute scorn and whispered
in absolute tenderness. It had been cackled and spat out, shouted in

openmouthed throaty laughter, or squeezed between clenched teeth in a bitter sneer. Somehow they were all still quoting the councilman, who had ruined his career by getting caught smoking crack in a motel room with a prostitute. It was only through the sheer force of repetition that they came to understand how its meaning had morphed so that somehow each of them had, at one time or another, become the bitch in question:

Bitch bitch bitch bitch bitch . . .

It's all there, in Ellory Montgomery's book. Part of the vast prelude to his story of redemption, currently available in hardcover: *An Etymology of Family Values.*

There He Go

(1995)

For Latonya and for a long time there was only one man who mattered. And he was simply the coolest, the absolute baddest man to ever straddle the up end of gravity. A picture snapped some forty years before she was born had given her all she thought she needed to know. In it, her granddaddy Clark was turning a corner in a finely tailored suit, smoothing out the concrete in a pair of patent leather shoes. A cigarette hung from his lower lip while rectangular shades blocked harsh streetlight from blurry nighttime eyes already, no doubt, stoned.

Whoever took the picture was actually aiming the camera at her great-uncle Martin, up in front and flashing a toothy grin while an anonymous, light-skinned girl hung off his left arm. Latonya could just barely make out her grandfather near the edge of the frame, a thin shadow turning a corner to join them, his image so faded behind the veil of smoke he himself was blowing that his features were barely recognizable.

That's all that was left of him. An old photograph she kept in her pocket for years and which only caught a glimpse of him in the background. Yet with one "look, there he go," passed on to her by her mother when she was nine, Latonya had been marked for life: the man she loved most was a gangster strut in badass shades, creeping up behind somebody.

"Look, there he go. . . ."

Latonya was nine and her whole family was busy moving boxes into their new apartment, having recently relocated from Fayetteville, North Carolina, to Atlanta, Georgia. They had already moved so many times by then that nobody bothered unpacking most things. Boxes were simply carted around from state to state, from apartment to apartment, without any of them remembering what most of those boxes actually were anymore except heavy. But every now and then something got dropped and some small but important piece of their lives would tumble out. That morning the bottom fell out of an armload of cardboard as Latonya's mother lifted it from the trunk of the car, unleashing a waterfall of warped blues albums that dribbled off the rear bumper and pooled around her ankles. She reached down and fished out a photograph wedged between Little Walter and Joe "Lemon Drop" Turner. She dusted it off and handed it to Latonya.

"That's your great-uncle Martin, the one who raised me back in Louisiana, the one your brother is named after. And there's your granddaddy Clark coming up behind him. You see him? Look, there he go—"

Latonya took the picture from her mother and brought it upstairs to the small bedroom she would be sharing with her brother for the next six months. She sat down on the edge of a still-bare mattress and stared at it for a good, long time.

After a while her grandfather's image must have seared itself into the static of Latonya's brain and would remain etched there for what seemed to her mother to be an eternity of adolescence. Old ladies who had known him crossed themselves out of instinct whenever Latonya entered a room as her mother spent the next five years carting her and her brother up and down the Eastern Seaboard. It seemed like there wasn't a single state in the Union where they didn't have some kind of people, and every house they entered had at least one old lady sitting on the couch, clutching a Bible, and watching soap operas with a shawl wrapped around her shoulders and a scrawny dog panting on her lap. Yet not even the flowery dresses and shiny shoes her mother stuffed Latonya inside, hot-combing her hair for family visits to ask for money or a temporary place to stay—no, not even pity could shield these old ladies from a phantom feeling of familiarity, a thin wisp of recognition, an uneasiness that wafted up the dog's nose and made it yap incessantly until Latonya's mother found another job or another man and the three of them—Mother, Latonya, and Martin—went back to wherever it was they came from.

"You know who that child takes after?" the old ladies whispered. But it had been so long since anyone had seen that fool or smelled his whiskey breath that they themselves could scarcely remember. Until Latonya opened her mouth. By the age of twelve the girl was already a habitual liar, but it took people a while to notice this because she only liked to talk about one thing.

Popping that faded photograph out of her pocket, Latonya spent a good portion of her childhood seated at somebody else's dinner table talking nonsense while, in the chair next to her, her mother was busy begging someone to loan them a couple dollars—and the only reason anyone ever did was from feeling sorry for her brother, Martin, with his sadly big head, eyes, and teeth being dragged across the country on the arm of two such frightful females.

"Look, there he go. That's my granddaddy," Latonya said proudly. Then proceeded to tell everybody what she had decided was the story of his life. As if no one else knew better, as if he belonged only to her.

Just one faded photograph had done that. Turned her mind into a palace of inspiration. A palace full of big empty rooms just as rat infested as her grandfather's last New York apartment had been. Oh, but Latonya swore she knew him. Claimed she was privy to all the intimate details of his life. Filled in the massive blanks of her origins with lies until she somehow came out his favorite grandchild. Conjured up an image so glorious and powerful that somehow she managed to manifest the look in his eyes.

Eddie Clark,
you got the spark
Run around breaking
all the young girls' hearts.
They know you wrong
but then you gone—
tell them that you love them
before you move on.
Why is it they always say
if you really got to go away
just tell me there's a chance
you'll be back someday.

"Girl, that old man wasn't nothing but a dope fiend, dropping his seed from here to St. Louis. He treated your grandmomma just like a dog. Wasn't anybody in that family any good except your great-uncle Martin, who you need to drop to your knees and thank Jesus for each and every night. He's the one that took care of your momma. And every time you pop that shameful picture in somebody's face and start telling stories you tarnish Martin's memory."

This was finally explained to Latonya when she was fourteen, by an old lady she met in Gainesville, Florida. The woman was so mean she wouldn't let Latonya or her mother set foot in her house anyway, but she took pity on Martin and was the one who wound up raising him. Nearly knocked all the daydream out of the girl by the time she got finished cussing everybody out. Latonya was so stunned by the loss of her grandfather that it took a while for her to notice that the woman was taking the only real man in her life away from her too.

"How old was he then?" The woman snatched the picture from Latonya's hands. "Thirty? I'm surprised he could still drag his sorry behind out of bed by then. Must have been all jazzed up about having Martin come to visit him. . . . Last time I saw him he was sitting on a bench in Washington Square Park, talking to himself. It was the middle of winter and he didn't have any socks on."

She handed the picture back to Latonya as her mother hugged and kissed Martin good-bye. Then the woman shut the door and her brother was gone.

After that Latonya became sullen. She stopped showing her picture to people and realized she didn't really have anything else to talk about. A few months later Latonya's mother settled down with a dishwasher repairman she'd met in Tampa. For the next few years Latonya got comments on her report cards like "doesn't participate in class" or "seems to have trouble getting adjusted to her new environment. She should be encouraged to take part in more after-school activities." But really, there wasn't a Girl Scout troop, cheerleading squad, or softball team anywhere in the state of Florida that could have fixed what ailed the girl at that point.

Latonya was fourteen, eyes already opened, consciousness already formed. It was too late to go back to sew up the frayed edge of the raggedy childhood her mother had given her and which she had only survived by staring at that photograph for so long. For as far back as she could remember, every time she looked up she saw nothing but chaos and neglect, a whizzing blur of trees and blue sky speeding past the open window of a moving car. Reality was just like the sunset or a father: always on its way out the door. So she'd formed lies as sweet as she could make them because she could not as yet see any point to the truth.

That last old lady who stole her brother more or less broke Latonya's heart. The next time Latonya dared take out her photograph
it had already started to look different to her. She could see that the
woman had been telling the truth. But how do you hate something
that is already a part of you? How do you become yourself without
betraying that same evil look in your own eyes?

My old man was easy
he gave me his last name
then stole my momma's money—
now ain't that a shame?
My old man was greedy
gave me nothing but a smile
and the sound of him leaving
while my momma cried.
My old man must have loved me
because he gave me his eyes
so I can see what you're up to
before you're fool enough to try.

Nevertheless, at sixteen Latonya gave birth to a fat baby boy she
named Willis, Junior, after his father.

Brother Martin, on the other hand . . .

• • •

BROTHER MARTIN, WHO WAS JUST like his namesake and never knew
any better than to love everybody, found himself laid up with a mean,
stingy old woman for the next three years. The first things she taught
him were the correct ways to do her dishes, fold her laundry, and
debone her fish. The last thing she taught him was how to properly
massage her feet. Then she promptly informed him that anything else
he needed to know he'd have to pick up on his own.

Of course Martin didn't actually *need* anything except his precious momma. He spent three years making up excuses for why she hadn't come back for him yet. While the old woman sat in her easy chair, watched soap operas, clutched her Bible, shook her head, and sighed.

But memories mold themselves to the shape of our will. The past keeps creeping along in dreams of need. It didn't matter what that old woman said or did. She could no more make that boy not miss his momma than she could erase his big teeth.

That's why, when he turned eighteen, Martin decided he would go find her himself. He packed his clothes and caught a bus to the town where she was living. Since nobody showed up to meet him at the station, it wasn't until he'd walked halfway to his mother's front door that it occurred to him that she probably hadn't bothered to tell her new husband about him. It would have made things easier, and since she had long since disgraced herself before every member of the family who had ever cared, there wasn't anyone to come around and tell that she actually had *two* children.

He knew it was true as soon as his mother opened the front door. He saw the frantic look in her eyes, the way she slumped forward like it hurt to hug him. He received her tepid embrace with the same sad expression she remembered from the last time they'd seen each other, a look that told the world there would always be somebody around to love him. And deep in her heart she knew that leaving him to massage some old woman's feet was probably the kindest thing she had ever done for either of her children.

Heartbroken, he asked, "Where is she?"

So that's how they met up again: on the day of Willis, Senior's parole board hearing. Latonya's baby's daddy was up for parole on the day Martin arrived. Martin turned a corner and saw his sister sitting on a metal bench outside the Center for Creative Unity with a Newport dangling from her lips and a fat baby bouncing on her knee. Black stockings, leather jacket, long fingers dipped in gold-plated acrylics. Frosted, overprocessed hair curling to one side of her face. In her last letter she'd told him she couldn't wait for Willis to get out of jail, but now that it was actually about to happen she was starting to have mixed feelings about it. . . .

The two of them took one look at each other and realized they'd spent their whole lives loving the wrong fools.

False Cognates

(1996)

1.

"I don't understand."

Mr. Richards removed the boy's paper from its folder and placed it on his desk. He looked up at the slender brown man in the ill-fitting suit fidgeting uncomfortably in the seat across from him. The boy's father, Mr. Jenkins, said:

"It's just, I know my son. . . . I mean, I know what he is capable of."

Mr. Richards nodded. Trying to explain to confused parents why their child had failed was surely the least pleasant of his duties as assistant dean of West Wesley Preparatory School. The situation was always that much more difficult when the boy in question was like this one and clearly bright. If troubled. Mr. Richards had reviewed the boy's file and was convinced that the mistakes in his current work were intentional. But they were still mistakes.

"Uncle J. was not a killer. He didn't even no that man. They thought they could frame him because he had a reputation, because the police new he sold drugs. But that didn't mean he was a killer. He just gave folks what they needed to dull the pane."

"Now, Mr. Jenkins, I want you to know that we at West Wesley do not consider these scores to reflect, in an absolute sense, your son's intelligence. But it is simply not possible for William to retain his current scholarship with grades like these."

"Uncle J. was smart. He always made a prophet."

He watched Mr. Jenkins wince and clutch his stomach. If the information on William's original application was correct, then Mr. Jenkins was an attorney of some sort. William was not, as he claimed, from "the streets" but rather the undesirable edge of a comfortable suburb, one of five African Americans carefully selected by the scholarship committee to walk the corridors of West Wesley without mop, spatula, or competitive benefits. Much of what the boy had written was therefore lies. But sometimes there was a deeper truth to lies, if only in the need for them.

"Walked out the wrong door one knight is all that happened. Turned down the wrong alley and saw something he wasn't supposed to sea. A mad swirl of dark shadows, clenched fists wrapped around pulled back triggers. A circle of seven angry gangsters and the barrel of a gun standing over an other man down."

"I have circled all the relevant passages so that—"
"I see them," Mr. Jenkins said. He picked up the paper and held it in front of his face.
Mr. Richards stared at a blank page.

"A lot of folks would have just kept walking if they saw something like that. A lot of folks would have turned and ran. But Uncle J.

wasn't like a lot of folks. He couldn't stand to see no man pray upon the week."

While Mr. Jenkins read, Mr. Richards considered his appearance: the jittery movements, the hunched shoulders, the frayed cuffs of his jacket. This was the fifth time this year a parent had been called in to discuss the boy's academic performance, yet it was only the first time Mr. Jenkins had seen fit to show up for the appointment. Usually the boy came with his mother. Mr. Richards knew from experience that very often when young boys took such precipitous downturns it was in response to negative stimuli in the home, a fact which made the decision to revoke the child's scholarship all the more heartless, his own relationship to that decision so untenable.

"Let me reiterate, Mr. Jenkins. This is not an expulsion. Should the boy's grades improve by the end of the semester, you have my assurance: I will personally see to it that his scholarship is reinstated."

"'Stay out of this,' those gangsters shouted and pointed to the won lying at their feat. 'This fool ain't nothing but a worthless junkie. He's knot your problem and this knot your fight.'"

"He's got a lot of words in here saying two things at once," Mr. Jenkins said finally.

Mr. Richards nodded. Actually, the words said three things. They told a story.

"What I mean is if you read it out loud, if you just listen to the sound of it, it makes perfect sense. So these are spelling errors but the logic is there."

Mr. Richards frowned. Clearly Mr. Jenkins had no intention of discussing what his son had actually written. Yet nothing happened in a vacuum. That, in fact, was the school's primary concern.

"Perhaps if you just let him rewrite it . . ."

"I can't do that. Quite frankly, there have been other incidents, minor disciplinary infractions, nothing serious in and of themselves. But given the violent imagery in some of your son's work . . . well, some of his teachers are concerned it might constitute a pattern."

This was an understatement. The boy's teachers were convinced he was a loose cannon and wanted to be rid of him altogether. If it weren't for Mr. Richards' efforts to intercede on the child's behalf, he would have been expelled.

"A pattern?"

"Blam! They tried to shoot him. Uncle J. dodged the bullet and Boom! Boom! Fought them off with his bear hand."

"Profits," Mr. Jenkins said softly. Like he was conceding something. "Profits and prophets . . ."

"Yes, Mr. Jenkins. Homophones."

And not even that, really. Mr. Jenkins kept saying fate, perhaps to emphasize his point. When really it was more like fit and fête. "False cognates can be tricky."

"But why do you think it's so confusing for him?"

Mr. Richards sighed. He looked at the hapless man across from him and all at once the full weight of the moment pressed in upon him. He'd read William's work, had reviewed his file. He was still convinced that the boy had enormous potential. Yet in a few moments Mr. Jenkins would gather his belongings, walk out the door, and that would be that. The matter would be completely out of Mr. Richards' control. Perhaps he would never see William again.

"Already he could here the sound of sirens behind him, police man coming with his flashing red lights. Those gangsters took off

running but it was too late. The man on the ground was already gone."

"You're not understanding me," Mr. Jenkins said. "I'm asking you an actual question. Perhaps it's some sort of cognitive development issue, one that has not been properly assessed as yet. Because it seems to me that most people couldn't even read a generation or two ago. Everything had to be sounded out. So how did they differentiate?"

"What?"

"Between profits and prophets."

A quote from Shakespeare popped into Mr. Richards' head: *You taught me language and my profit on it* . . .

"I'm asking you what you *think*."

Mr. Richards winced. "I think, Mr. Jenkins, that to let your son rewrite this paper, to reinstate his scholarship without consequence, would be tantamount to a form of theft. It would not be fair to the other students, and quite frankly, it would not be fair to your son."

He rose to his feet.

"Go home, Mr. Jenkins. Tell your son to look up false cognate in the dictionary. Then consider your options very carefully. Because I sincerely believe there is still a place for William at West Wesley. But he needs to understand that there are consequences for his actions. Just like everyone else's."

Mr. Richards waited for Mr. Jenkins to leave his office. Then he sat back down and brooded over the unpleasantness of his duties as assistant dean.

He was still an educator, after all. When was the calling more profound than when presented with a student like this one? The boy had talent; it took talent for an eighth grade boy to fail with such resolution, and Mr. Richards perceived this, was not so circumscribed by his duties as assistant dean that he no longer recognized art. But what

if he was the only one who saw it? What if he was the father figure the
boy so clearly needed? The steady hand, the guiding glance. The push.

> *"They said he was the killer and took him to jail. The man who
> razed me, only Papa I ever new."*

He could feel himself becoming agitated and sought solace in a
picture of a smiling young woman he had placed on his desk years before: his wife. He stared at the photograph for a long time, trying very
hard to focus on a single point, the glint in the woman's eye.

> *"A misunderstanding was all it was. All Uncle J. was trying to do
> that knight was keep the piece."*

He blinked.

2.

So I'm a drug dealer now, Douglas Jenkins thought. He shoved his son's
paper into the pocket of his jacket and walked down a long hall, still
struggling to make sense of what just happened. He'd lost an argument, although it hadn't been much of one. Now he had to go home
and tell his mother that William had lost his scholarship. Other ar-
rangements would have to be made.

A group of boys marched by in uniform and Douglas looked down
at the floor, at the hem of his pants sagging over his shoes, laces skid-
ding across the tiles in counter rhythm to his footsteps. He was wearing one of his old suits that his mother had kept for him, but somehow
it didn't fit anymore; when he put it on that morning she'd muttered
something about him needing time to grow back into it. Then she'd
smiled, straightened his tie, and pushed him out the door. As if com-

ing to West Wesley to talk to his son's assistant dean was just the first in a series of simple tasks that led to him getting his life back, and soon enough everything would be like before.

Douglas had kissed his mother's cheek just like he had shaken the dean's hand and then made sure to look the man straight in the eye. All the while aware that every gesture, every word from his mouth would be interpreted as the attempted correction of a misunderstanding he was not responsible for. Because what his son had written was not Douglas's story. He was no one's Uncle J. Yet he had spent three months behind bars due to a single night in some ways similar to the one the boy described. Except Douglas wasn't a drug dealer. He was an attorney. And it wasn't a prison where he'd served the majority of his sentence. It was a psychiatric ward.

Furthermore, the police were already there.

Douglas stopped walking. A terrible thought occurred to him. What if there was actually something wrong with William? Some synaptic breach in his nervous system, something passed down paternally?

But then he remembered that couldn't have been it. Whatever else was wrong with Douglas, he'd always done well in school. If he'd passed along anything it would have been perfectionism, an obsessive need to exceed others' expectations. He had been diagnosed with obsessive-compulsive disorder, among other things. It had been explained to him several times during the past year that that was why he was so easily agitated, why he didn't always know when to leave well enough alone.

He pushed through a heavy wooden door and passed into the bright sunlight of the afternoon. He walked to the corner, sat on a bench, and watched a man push a mower across a rolling green lawn. Another group of children ran by, book bags bouncing on their shoulders as they jostled and pushed each other down the block.

As Douglas watched them make their way across the street

another possibility roared through his mind. What if William was stupid? Too stupid to understand the opportunity he'd been given, too stupid to do the work required to maintain his place?

He took a deep breath. If William was stupid then surely Douglas could not be held responsible. That was something the boy must have inherited from his mother.

Douglas's ex-wife, the boy's mother, was perhaps the only one who'd never believed there was anything wrong with Douglas. The one person who'd never wavered in her faith that he had not, as the police claimed, suffered some sort of drug-induced psychosis that night. No, instead she was furious, convinced he had done it with the sole intent of publicly humiliating *her*. How else to explain how a man of his intelligence would allow a misdemeanor charge of public urination to escalate into a felony altercation with the police?

All he'd been trying to do that night was take a pee. He'd gone to Henry's Bar with his brother after work and at some point needed to use the bathroom. The urinal was broken, so he stepped outside. Walked out the wrong door, turned down the wrong alley. Saw something he wasn't supposed to see. A man on the ground being struck repeatedly by two police officers. Yet it was clear that the suspect, if that was what he was, had already been subdued. There was no reason to hit him anymore.

Douglas had spoken without thinking, been punched in the groin for his trouble, and when he continued to protest, he was hauled off to jail. There he'd remained for the next twelve hours, at which point he was informed that the only one who'd be facing criminal charges was him. Because they were in him: the drugs. He knew that they were, even before they demanded he take the blood test.

Just like he knew what he had seen.

A bus pulled up to the curb. Douglas waited until the doors opened then stood up and reached into his pocket. He found the coins his mother had given him, dropped them into a metal slot, and made his way down the aisle. He found a seat and stared out the window, watching still more children move up and down the sidewalk.

They're like little inkblots, Douglas thought. Like the ones they'd shown him before his competency hearing: *"Tell me what you see. . . ."*

Who knew how long his life might have gone on the way it had been if it wasn't for that night? Getting dressed for work each morning, kissing his wife at the door, smiling before his superiors and snorting coke only every now and then at his desk behind a locked door. Walking among his coworkers without ever really being (in truth he was always vaguely aware of this) wholly present.

The bus pulled to a stop near the entrance to the park and Douglas climbed down. He walked past the Byrdie's Burgers on the corner and made his way through the park, stopping when he happened to see his old dealer rolling a cigarette as he sat perched on the railing of a bench. He raised the cigarette to his lips and drew the edge of the paper along his tongue. When he saw Douglas he smiled in recognition and nodded to an orange fanny pack strapped around his waist.

Douglas frowned. They'd sucked all the secrets out of him that night, drained his life like blood from a needle. He'd lost his job, his wife, and his license to practice law had been suspended. All that was left was an encroaching sense of oblivion and an overwhelming desire to get high. The only problem was how to pay for it. He didn't have money or anything else to offer anyone anymore.

But he knew where he could get it.

"I'll be right back," he said. Then he turned around, walked to the end of the block, and climbed the steps to his mother's front door.

He found her in the kitchen, dressed in a housecoat and slippers, hips shaking in jagged spasms as she stood over the stove beating an egg in a small ceramic bowl. When she heard Douglas come in she turned around and smiled.

"What did the man say, Doug?"

Douglas looked away from her, towards the living room: the

sea-foam-colored shag carpet, the green paisley print wallpaper, the low couch where his brother Daryl now sat, watching TV. Towering above the entire room was a life-size portrait of Douglas's father back in his pro boxing days, bare-chested and glove-fisted as he crouched beneath a banner that bore what had been his professional moniker before he retired from the ring, settled down, and married Douglas's mother. The Brown Bomber.

Everything looked exactly the way it had when Douglas was growing up.

"Doug? Did you talk to him? Get it all straightened out?"

Except for the tarp. Shortly after his father passed, his mother began wrapping the room in plastic as a way to keep it clean for those rare occasions when company came to visit. Plastic runners crisscrossed the carpet, plastic covers enveloped the cushions of the couch, plastic sheeting draped the front of the glass-doored cabinet that was stuffed to bursting with souvenirs from his father's career. Things that had sat untouched for years, things his mother couldn't even be bothered to dust anymore. Things that could have been sold to help pay for Douglas's appeal.

He looked at his mother. "It's all kind of mucked up at this point, Ma. I didn't get back in time. The boy lost his scholarship and I can't afford the tuition right now. You know very well it's going to take some time for me to get back on my feet."

His mother gasped. "You mean he's been expelled?"

She was watching him the way his son used to in his old life, whenever he went out of town for a legal conference then came home and realized the boy had been expecting some sort of present. Like a child who'd been disappointed before.

"Not exactly. The assistant dean said he was welcome to continue. I just have to pay for it."

"Well, what does that mean? Some kind of payment plan?"

He looked around the living room. His mother was basically living in a mausoleum wrapped in plastic. Yet they both knew that there was thousands of dollars' worth of memorabilia in the cabinet alone.

"We might have to sell some of Papa's stuff."

"What? You want me to sell Papa?"

"It's not Papa, Ma." Douglas shook his head. "It's Papa's stuff. I've told you before, people remember Papa and some of them would pay a lot of money for these things you've got here. If we sold just a few of them we could probably get enough to cover the boy's tuition. And Dean Richards promised William could get his scholarship back if he improves next term."

"You believe that?" Daryl shouted from the couch. "Why should Ma pay all that money to send the boy to some fancy private school when he doesn't even want to go?"

Douglas frowned. It was still hard to look at his brother and not think about the night of his arrest. Daryl, after all, was the one who had insisted Douglas meet him at Henry's.

We never see each other anymore. Just come out for a couple of hours, it will be like old times. Unless you don't want to hang out with me now that you—

"I wasn't talking to you, Daryl."

"Yeah, well, I'm talking to you."

Daryl set his beer down on a vinyl cloth draped across the coffee table and stood up. He was still wearing his green uniform from work.

"Did it ever occur to either of you geniuses that maybe he's just tired of being the only Black kid at that school? It's got him feeling all alienized and, can I be real for a minute? I think it's starting to affect his mind."

"Hush," their mother said. She pointed towards the ceiling. "The boy can hear you, you know."

Douglas glared at his brother. He still remembered the look on Daryl's face that night, when he ran outside and found Douglas propped against the hood of that police car. The way he stopped and stepped backwards, telling Douglas to be cool and not to worry. He said he'd meet him at the city jail with bail money and—

"Just stay out of this, Daryl. It doesn't concern you."

"Bullshit it doesn't. Who do you think was looking out for the boy while you were gone, Doug? Me and Ma, that's who. You can tell your snooty ex-wife I said so too. She doesn't pay any attention to that child now that she's got her new man. Just so long as he doesn't get in her way. Ask Ma."

"Quiet," their mother said. "Don't talk so loud."

"William needs to go to school right here, Doug. Be around his own people for a change. I mean I understand you just want what's best for him, but fuck. . . . Look what they did to you."

Douglas turned back to his mother.

"Ma? Are you listening to me? Did you hear what I said? Because it's really quite simple. Either we find a way to pay or William will have to go to school somewhere else. Do you understand?"

"I think so, son." She stared at the portrait of The Brown Bomber and sighed. "You want me to sell Papa. . . ."

Douglas shook his head. *Oblivion*, he thought.

He stared at The Brown Bomber's gloved fists.

"I'll be right back," he said. Then turned around and marched up the stairs.

When he reached the second floor he walked down a dark hall to the bedroom where he and his brother had grown up. William was in there now; his ex-wife had consented to weekly visitations and Douglas could hear the boy talking to someone on the phone. He leaned forward and squinted through the crack in the door, saw the boy's legs swinging over the edge of a messy bed as he wound the phone's cord around and around his forearm, another poster of his father glaring back at him from the boy's closet door.

Douglas stared at the poster. *If only Papa was still here*, Douglas thought. The Brown Bomber would have known what to do. The

Brown Bomber, who had lived his life as if he truly believed he could smooth out the entire world with the force of his fist and the flat of his palm.

He took a deep breath and pushed through the door just as his son was hanging up the receiver.

"Who was that?"

"Mr. Richards."

"The dean? He calls you at home?"

"I guess."

Douglas squinted. "Isn't that . . . strange? I mean it seems a bit invasive, doesn't it? Inappropriate, to contact you at home?"

"I don't know. Honestly, he's never done it before. He said he just wanted to tell me how much he hopes I'll be back next year. He thinks I have potential, whatever that means. He said he liked my paper."

"That's what he said?"

Back in Mr. Richards' office Douglas had said there was a logic to what William had written, but that was just the lawyer in him, trying to plead a case.

"What else does Mr. Richards say to you?"

"I don't know." The boy shrugged. "The usual stuff . . ."

"The usual stuff? Is there a reason he can't talk to you about the usual stuff during school hours?"

"Not if I'm not going to school there anymore. He wants me to stay at West Wesley, says I need to buckle down and do my work so I can realize my full potential. He said he hates thinking about me winding up just another statistic."

"A statistic, huh?" Douglas nodded. He sat down on the edge of the bed next to his son and stared at the poster of The Brown Bomber, shirtless and gleaming as he clenched his fists and somehow managed to snarl and smile at the same time.

"You know, son. I realize that there are a lot of things we haven't really had a chance to talk about yet. But the truth is . . . Well. Sometimes Caucasians can get some pretty wild ideas about what Black people are like, the things we are capable of. That's why we have to be very careful that our gestures are not misinterpreted." He looked at the poster of his father and thought back to the night of his arrest, the young man he'd seen lying on the ground. "I'm telling you it's dangerous."

"What do you mean, Dad?"

"That story you wrote. I can't help but wonder if, perhaps subconsciously . . . Do you think that when you wrote it you were just trying to say what you thought that man wanted to hear?"

"Who? Mr. Richards?"

"I'm only asking because I know you."

"No, you don't."

"I mean I know what you are capable of," Douglas said. "You know better than to make mistakes like that. And all that stuff about drug dealers and gangsters. You don't associate with people like that. You weren't raised that way. Why would you feel the need to write about things like that?"

William looked down at his shoe. He pushed his fingers through the laces and wound the bow around and around his thumb. He shook his head.

"Truth?"

"Well, of course. I'm your father, you can tell me anything."

"I don't want to go back there."

Douglas nodded. He placed his hand on his son's back. "Son, I know it's difficult now. But one day—"

"No, I mean I'm *not* going back," the boy said. "I want to go to school right here, in the neighborhood. I already told Mr. Richards, and when Mom comes to take me home, I'm going to tell her too."

Douglas stared at his son. He realized he'd forgotten again. It was not his decision anymore. He no longer had custody, and he didn't have the money to keep the boy in school and they both knew it. So what the hell were they even talking about?

Oblivion, Douglas thought. He stood up.

"Wait, Dad, where are you going?"

"I'll be back."

He walked out of the room and shut the door behind him, then stood alone on the other side, listening to the sound of the TV downstairs.

So William had done it on purpose, let those people at that school think he was a fool in an effort to have his way. Douglas would have never dared do something so stupid as a boy because he knew his father would have beaten his ass. The Brown Bomber had ruled over his family with an iron fist, but Douglas always told himself he would be a different kind of father, just like he'd worked so hard to be his own man. And what did he have to show for it? He'd lost his career, his wife, and, apparently, control of his own son. All because something inside him would not allow him to lie about what he'd seen. It was a willful act, an assertion of selfhood that, because it seemingly occurred within a void, gave the entire turn of events an air of self-destruction, the illusion of choice. What kind of choice was his son making, he wondered. What had he taught his son about what it took to survive this world? Or what survival even meant?

After a while he wiped his eyes, took a deep breath, and walked down the hall until he reached his parents' immaculate bedroom.

As he pushed through the door his heart pounded, a sensation Douglas instantly recognized as a strangely soothing vestige of the fear he'd felt as a child whenever he entered his parents' room without permission. He walked to the edge of the bed and got down on his knees as memories of his father's voice ran through him like a shiver.

"What the hell do you think you're doing in my room, boy?"

Douglas used to wince in fear every time he heard his father call his name, but those were also the days when everything felt simple and safe, The Brown Bomber's heavy hand hanging over everything like cloud cover. The man had been a groundskeeper for as far back as Douglas could remember but, lest anyone forget there had been a before, the entire house was a monument to someone who'd been strong enough to fight their way out of some saltwater slum with their bare hands.

"And I'll beat the fool out of you too, if that's what it takes."

Douglas threw back the edge of the comforter and felt around underneath the bed until he found a large hatbox. He pulled it towards him and removed the top. Inside it was an enormous pair of boxing gloves. He reached inside one and removed the small pearl-handled pistol that had been stuffed into the palm.

"Don't even think about messing with my things. You hear me, boy? Cuz I will beat the tar outta you."

He set the pistol on the floor and turned the glove over. A heart-shaped diamond brooch, a gold watch, and a dozen stray bullets tumbled onto the floor like spare change.

"I will beat the stupid."

He put the first glove down, reached inside the second, and pulled out a fat roll of cash tied up in a gold money clip.

"I will beat the ugly."

In truth Douglas had known where his parents hid their emergency stash of cash since he and his brother were twelve and ten years old, but he would have never dared touch it while his father was alive. Now he removed the clip and counted out nine hundred dollars. It wasn't enough to pay the boy's tuition, but it meant there were options. Enough for a decent suit, enough for a bus ticket out of town, enough to get his hands on whatever that man in the park had hidden in his fanny pack . . .

Douglas hadn't yet decided what it was he needed most.

"You hear me, boy?"

Douglas looked down at his father's glove. *Profits and prophets,* he thought. As different as he and The Brown Bomber may have been, he was still his father's son, a product of how he'd been raised. That was why it didn't matter what they did to him or how much the truth cost him. He was never going to lie about what he'd seen. In part it was because he was a good man, an honorable man, a man who, despite his many flaws, tried to do the right thing. But it was also because he knew what The Brown Bomber would have done to him if he ever found out Douglas had backed down from a fight.

"Now get up off your knees, son. Act like you got some pride."

Douglas shoved the money into his pants pocket then put the pistol back in the glove and pushed the hatbox under the bed. He smoothed down the comforter and stood up just in time to hear the click of a door closing behind him.

"Son?" Douglas said and got no response.

HE'D BARELY MADE IT HALFWAY down the stairs when a voice called out, "It's all right you know," which was followed by the low squeal of plastic. When he looked in the living room Daryl was still sitting on the couch, head pivoted away from the TV and smiling at him.

"I mean there's nothing wrong with William if that's what you're worried about. He just doesn't want to go to that school anymore."

"How do you know?"

"He told me." Daryl shrugged. "He tells me a lot of things. He and I talk."

"Is that right?"

"Well, of course. Just trying to be a good uncle. And now that you're back . . . I want you to know that I'm here for you, Douglas. I mean that. Take you to meetings, whatever you need. You just let me know."

Douglas nodded. He thought about the way Daryl had smiled at him that night at the bar, the way he'd laughed when he'd pulled that pipe from his pocket.

"*Relax, Doug. Let's have ourselves a good time. You're not at work and your wife's not here. It's just me, remember? Your brother.*"

Here was a man who could handle his high. An uncle . . .

Douglas reached into his pocket. "Why don't you help me with this."

"What is it?"

"William's story, the one he turned in at school. Maybe you can make sense of it, seeing as how the two of you are so close."

He stood near the couch and watched his brother's lips move as his eyes scanned the page.

After a while, Daryl said, "That's crazy," and put the paper down. He looked at Douglas. "What?"

"I'm just trying to figure out where he got this stuff from."

"Well, why are you looking at me like that? Doug?"

"Did you tell my son I was a drug dealer?"

Daryl frowned. "I knew it." He shook his head. "That's just typical, isn't it? Everything's got to be my fault. Right, Doug? No matter what happens, you always got to find some way to blame me."

"What's going on out there?" their mother shouted from the kitchen.

"I mean, here you are, one foot out of the fucking nuthouse and you're going to try to make it my fault that your kid is screwed up?"

"What are you saying?" Their mother walked out wiping her hands on her apron. She smiled towards the ceiling. "He's not screwed up. Nobody in this house is screwed up. Why would you say a thing like that?"

"You're missing the point, Ma. Which, by the way, is also typical. The point is Doug's trying to blame *me*."

"Just answer the question, Daryl," Douglas said. "Did you tell my son I was a drug dealer or not?"

"Your son?"

"Yes. My son."

Daryl shook his head. He looked at his mother. He looked back at Douglas.

"Fuck, Doug. No . . . I mean, of course not. I mean, I may have said some things. But nothing like what he wrote there."

Douglas turned to his mother. "Are you hearing this?"

His mother frowned. "Yes, son. I hear it."

Then why don't you do something, Douglas thought. *Why won't you help me?*

"It's like this, see? You were gone and we didn't even know when you were coming back. Naturally your son—*my* nephew—has got a lot of questions. And the truth is it's fucking sad. I mean, no offense, but that's the truth of it, it's just fucking sad. So I might have told him . . . some things. Just trying to prop you up a little bit. Trying to turn a negative into a positive some kind of way. Give him a little something to work with. I guess he must have got confused somehow. . . ."

"So better to be a drug dealer than a so-called addict? Is that what you mean?"

"Yeah, so-called. Something like that." Daryl shook his head. "Why not?"

Douglas stared at his brother. He could feel his heart pound in his chest as scattered memories of the night of his arrest swirled in his mind like a flock of startled birds. There he was, back in that dark alley, staring at a redbrick wall. Thinking about all the work he still had to do when he got home, thinking about how he was going to explain that to Daryl without hurting his feelings. That it had nothing to do with the company, it was simply time to call it a night.

"You feel better now, Douglas? Is that what you wanted to hear?"

Next thing he knew there was a strange sound behind him: a thump, a muffled gasp, the shuffling of feet. And somehow he felt compelled to turn around.

"Of course I didn't tell him those things about you. What, just because you lost it you think I'm crazy too? You're fucked up, man. Fucked up for even asking me that question. I just didn't want him to think you were just a victim, man, another statistic. I don't know where he got that other stuff from."

There he was, in the back seat of a police car. Bouncing over potholes as the sound of his own gasps merged with the wail of sirens, the flashing lights, the voices from the front—

Bastard junkie nigger sit

—all hurtling him towards the blank wall of the now.

"I'm on your side. It's me, Doug. Remember? Your brother."

Douglas balled his fist. He lurched forward and stumbled over an extension cord; the goose-necked lamp fell to the floor as Daryl stepped backwards and flinched.

"Watch yourself now, Doug. Don't lose your cool."

Douglas gripped the collar of Daryl's shirt with his left hand and swung wildly with his right. The impact of the blow knocked his brother against the cabinet of souvenirs. The unsheathed Brown Bomber stared down at his two sons as the glass door shook and shattered and the tarp fell across their bodies like a veil.

"Stop!" their mother cried.

Douglas squinted at his brother crouched beneath him, pieces of glass flickering like stardust in his hair, the lower half of his face smeared with blood bubbling from his nose.

Like little inkblots, Douglas thought and raised his fist.

3.

William Jenkins stood on the front porch of Mr. Richards' house, still unsure about whether he should have come. He was just about to retreat down the front steps when the door opened and Mr. Richards appeared.

"William? What are you doing here?"

"I changed my mind," William stammered. "I want to stay in school, take advantage of this opportunity to make something of myself."

"Well, good," Mr. Richards said. "But it doesn't entirely answer my question."

He looked around the quiet street. "How did you find my address?"

"I looked it up in the yellow pages. Wasn't hard to figure out where you live, where your wife works . . ."

"You shouldn't have done that. It's quite the violation . . . of privacy. You should come to my office during school hours."

"I can't if I'm not going to school there. Anyhow, you called me at home, so I figured it was okay. I just wanted to tell you I want to stay. I'm willing to put the work in to make good grades, start acting right, take my assignments seriously. Want to take advantage of this opportunity to make something of myself. Don't want to be just another statistic."

"Well, I'm glad to hear that. I do believe that if you apply yourself, nothing can stop you from achieving your goals. If your father can just come up with the money—"

"Awww, he doesn't have any money," William said. "Mr. Richards? All that stuff I wrote? None of it's true. I don't have an Uncle J. My dad is the only one I know who's ever been to jail, and he's not a drug dealer. He just had a nervous breakdown and lost his job is all. . . . He's just plain crazy."

"Well, I am sorry to hear that." Mr. Richards sighed. "On the other hand, I'm glad you trust me enough to—"

"I've got something though. I found it in a hatbox under my grandparents' bed. It's what you call memorabilia. Probably worth a lot of money, maybe enough to pay my tuition."

"Is that right?"

"It's why I came over. I want to show it to you."

Mr. Richards glanced back inside the house. His wife appeared in the hall, arms folded in front of her chest.

He turned back to William. "Son, I don't think that now is the right time to—"

"Just have a look at it will you?"

Mr. Richards sighed. He stepped out onto the porch and shut the door behind him.

"All right, son. What is it?"

William smiled and reached into his pocket.

Yams

(1997)

Just then they were all eating yams, candied and still hot from the stove. Golden-brown pieces glistening with sauce that dripped from the serving spoon as it moved between the bowl and the plates. Heavy sweet pieces that clung to their forks, sank and settled on their tongues, and then dissolved in a swirl of rich textures.

The girl's uncle Todd pushed back his chair and reached for the bowl and a second helping. His broad hands pressed across the table, past his water glass and the ladle of gravy, the tea lights and decorative poinsettia, up and over the enormous ham.

"Why can't you just ask?"

The girl looked up and saw her uncle Richard glaring at his brother as he held up a glass of iced tea. She had two uncles; Uncle Richard always sat on the opposite side of the table between his wife, Aunt Ruth, and his daughter, Cousin Simone. Todd always sat next to his sister, the girl's mother.

Uncle Todd seized the bowl with both hands. He lifted it high above the table before he realized it was still hot. His arms shuddered in a quick spasmodic jerk as the bowl tilted and dipped between his fingers.

"The ham!" the girl's mother gasped. But Uncle Todd did not drop the bowl. He jiggled it between his fingers for a moment and then yanked it towards himself like a quick intake of breath, setting it down hard on the table.

"That's what the tongs are for," Aunt Ruth said.

Uncle Todd dunked the spoon into the bowl and dumped a large portion of yams onto his plate. Uncle Todd was her uncle who seemed convinced that if he waited for tongs he would only find that he was still hungry and perhaps that there was nothing left.

At the head of the table, the girl's grandfather asked for more iced tea. The pitcher was passed down, every hand moving slowly and deliberately as if offering a demonstration of how such things were properly done.

"Margaret called today," her grandfather said. "You get that message?"

"What did she want?" Uncle Todd said. He was her uncle who had quarreled with his wife and was currently sleeping on her grandparents' couch.

"To wish you a happy holiday, I imagine. How are things coming along, anyway? Everything all right?"

"It is what it is," Uncle Todd said. "I mean I'm still here, aren't I? Haven't given up yet."

Uncle Todd was her uncle who talked with his mouth full and then spit when he talked, sometimes slinging great gobs of half-masticated yams right onto the table. He turned his head and noticed the girl was staring. Mistaking her expression but noticing the lull in the conversation, something inside of him must have resolved to fill it.

He put down his fork and wiped his hands on his pants. He reached for the spoon and scooped out the last large piece of yam. He swung his arm across her mother's chest and held the spoon over the girl's plate.

"Here," Uncle Todd said.

The girl covered her plate with her hands and shook her head.

"No, thank you," she said. She told him that she'd had enough and was already full.

"Eat them anyway," Uncle Todd said and tipped his spoon. The only thing that saved her from burning the backs of her hands was a sudden instinct to flinch.

"What are you doing?" the girl's mother said.

Uncle Todd told the girl to eat her yams. He told her it was important to eat yams because it prevented sickle cell anemia. Years later, as a grown woman, she would be sitting in a doctor's office, thumbing through a medical journal, and she would come across an article that offered the far more plausible explanation that sickle cell had developed in Africa as a defensive response to the threat of malaria. But that night she sat and listened as her uncle talked about dietary deficiencies and the need for little Black girls to eat yams.

Uncle Todd told the girl that yams had been a staple of the West African diet, that her ancestors had eaten them the same way Asians eat rice. In Africa, yams were not something you only hauled out on holidays and special occasions, set among the fixtures of the slave diet her grandfather insisted brought good luck at Thanksgiving. The mustard greens, the black-eyed peas, the pickled pigs' feet, all crowded into smaller side dishes and placed around the enormous ham, that monument to all they had to be thankful for. Unlike these other things, the yam was no mere tribute to endurance in the face of deprivation and the beneficence of strong spice. The yam was something her ancestors had smuggled with them from Africa, like wisdom.

The girl stared at Uncle Todd and said nothing. He was her uncle who every Christmas gave her ugly digital watches that doubled as calculators. She ate her yams, accepted her inoculation to the extent that it tasted good.

"You hear that?" Uncle Richard said. "And all this time I just thought I liked the taste."

"It's a craving. Something we had to learn to do without."

"You sure about that, brother?" the girl's mother said. "Sure it's not the sugar?"

"No," Uncle Todd said. "It's not the sugar, it's not the salt. Just think of all the things that were lost or that we had to leave behind, never knowing if we would ever see them again. This yam, in a sense, is a symbol of our faith, a symbol of who we are."

Uncle Todd explained that Black Americans had survived their craving for yams and that like every other trial and deprivation they had endured during slavery it had helped to make them strong. He told her this was one of the great ironies of history, that the enslaved had wound up stronger than the enslaver, precisely because they had been bred that way.

"For crissakes," Aunt Ruth said. "I'm trying to eat. Can't you think of something more pleasant to talk about at the dinner table?"

"It's the truth," Uncle Todd said. "It's history, you can't blame me for history. Anyhow, you should be proud. Just try to imagine all your ancestors went through. All those generations that struggled to keep going, to find the strength to keep believing there was a reason to carry on no matter what."

Uncle Todd told Aunt Ruth that she should enjoy her yams and appreciate the fact that she deserved them. Because she was fit.

A silence swept across the table as if they were all deliberating the things he said. Uncle Todd was her uncle who, so far as the girl could tell, lived his life as a series of scams and get-rich-quick schemes. Sometimes he was her prosperous uncle and other times he was her uncle in a rumpled suit, staring across the table with bloodshot eyes, beseeching his siblings for "start-up capital." He was her uncle who sent postcards from South America, who had investments in Venezuela and El Salvador. He was her uncle who was currently being sued by the US government for tax evasion. But above all he was her uncle who talked so much it was impossible to dismiss the things he said as merely an excuse to distract everyone else from the more obvious questions he might have taken their silences to imply. For example: When was he going home to his wife?

"These are things I shouldn't have to tell you," Uncle Todd said. They wouldn't teach the girl these things in school, which was why she had to learn to read between the lines, just like it was natural for Black people to dance between beats. This was the key to Black creativity and also why Black children needed to be spanked.

Somehow yams had something to do with why Black children were so prone to hyperactivity. Their first impulse was always jittery and dreamy-eyed, as if they were missing something, looking for something, and worse still, actually believed they would find it. All of which was a consequence of slavery and made sense if you considered the resources that had been necessary to survive it. The strength of will, the sheer imagination required to keep believing there could be a way out of even the most oppressive situation, and therefore a need to keep going. It was why they had emerged as such a creative people.

This was especially true of the girl's ancestors, the North Carolina Negroes. Ever heard of Stagville? Right there in Durham? If the girl ever took the time to study her history she would know that Stagville once functioned, more or less, as a vast penal colony for problem slaves, the ones who could not be broken and kept running away. A certain type of white master would sell them off to Stagville where they would find themselves one among hundreds of slaves, surrounded by miles and miles of land bordered by armed guards.

Uncle Todd said, "They'd plop them down right in the middle and say, 'Okay, Negro. Let's see you run now. Let's see if you can even figure out which way is up.' That was how they thought they could finally break them. But of course that isn't what happened at all."

"Yes, that last shackle, the shackle of confusion," Aunt Ruth said. "That sounds about right."

"It's been the hardest one of all," Uncle Todd said.

The girl heard a gagging sound, looked up, and saw her cousin

Simone holding up her glass of water, saw the startled expression on Simone's face as something went down the wrong pipe.

"You all right?" Uncle Todd said.

Uncle Todd was her uncle who drove too fast on the highway, bulldozed over speed bumps, and then laughed as the girl and her cousin let out a series of terrified shrieks from the back seat. And when he slowed down, the girl and Simone always looked at each other, startled by the sound of their own voices as some nameless impulse of adrenaline caused them both to shout, "Again! Again!"

How did she think they had survived? And why did she think there were so many Black Americans with Native American blood? Because it was unnatural for a Black man to contemplate suicide. Their will to live was too strong because it had had to be. And that was why—

"All right, that's enough," Uncle Richard said. He threw his napkin down and stood up from the table. "Dammit, Todd. Just stop. If you need help that bad, just ask for it. But don't do this. Don't ruin dinner."

"Why do you always have to take things too far?" Aunt Ruth said. She picked up her husband's plate and followed him into the kitchen.

The girl stared at her uncle Todd. He was her uncle who, when she was four, snuck into her bedroom one night while she was sleeping and rubbed pepper on her thumb to get her to stop sucking it.

She narrowed her eyes.

"Who wants pie?" Aunt Ruth called from the kitchen.

"Eat your yams. They're good for you."

That night she just sat there, eating her yams because they tasted good, wondering why that wasn't good enough. She needed to be spanked, Uncle Todd said. All Black children did. Taught to respect their elders, to keep their eyes where they belonged, their hands where you could see them. Taught to obey the rules, made to understand how the world really worked. They needed to be spanked before it was too late, before their wild visions and mad cravings got the better of them and then they wound up ruined. Because when that happened there was only the family to blame.

While the girl's mother sat and stared and thought, *What if some of it is true? Not all of it, of course. But some of it and just enough.* She'd spent years trying to prove her brother wrong, chipping away at the idea that what the girl needed was a strong male role model. Meanwhile the girl was getting bigger by the day, more stubborn, more difficult to control. More like her father, who'd had so much potential once, only to wind up another man gone.

What if she just admitted it, that she wasn't always sure she could handle the girl alone? What if she just pushed back her chair, got up and out of Todd's way? What if she—

YEARS LATER, THE GIRL WAS still convinced that the only thing that saved her was a sudden instinct to flinch.

Houston and
the Blinking What

(1998)

Houston.

They were supposed to be helping out, taking some of the pressure off an old woman in her time of grief, but somehow it didn't feel that way. It felt like they were taking advantage, although Lynette liked to tell herself that after her uncle Leon died she and her husband Curtis might have offered to come stay with Aunt Trudy even if they had had some place else to go. She liked to tell herself a lot of things, but by the end of the third month even she couldn't hide from the suspicion that her aunt understood more about why they'd left Houston than she led on. Lynette knew her aunt Trudy, knew how hard the woman's life had been and the kind of person she was because of that. And so a part of Lynette also knew that the only thing that would have kept her aunt from asking them for rent money was if she'd already figured out that they didn't have it. That Lynette and the man she'd defied the entire family by marrying had made a mess of things, were broke, and that was the real reason they'd come home.

And just look what he'd done now.

"You fucked up my auntie's door," Lynette said. They were up in the bedroom, Lynette standing in front of the closet, one hand on her hip and the other holding back a curtain of clothes as she stared at the three-foot-high wooden door in the wall behind it, the shiny new bolt lock sealing it shut.

"What?" Curtis said, slumped on the edge of the bed behind her, a bottle of whiskey balanced between his knees and the saxophone he hadn't played in months lying in its case at his feet. "What are you complaining about now?"

"Come look."

"I don't want to look. Jesus, Lynette. What do you want from me? I packed up your uncle's books didn't I? I even fixed the lock."

"That's what I'm talking about," Lynette said. "The lock. You put it on the wrong side."

"No. That's how it was before. Just new is all. Old one was all rusted out. You're just confused because of the color."

But Lynette wasn't talking about the color. Throughout her childhood, whenever she and her sister, Stephanie, came to visit their aunt Trudy, the secret room at the back of the closet had been their favorite place to play. And even before they were old enough to understand what the room meant they'd sensed it meant something: not every house had secret rooms in the backs of their closets. When they were old enough their mother sat them down and explained it: how their uncle Leon wasn't in jail because he was a criminal; he was a political prisoner. How back in the seventies he'd started an organization that fought for the community and against police brutality. How in the years that followed the house had been raided on three separate occasions by authorities claiming to be looking for something that just wasn't there. The room was built so he and his allies would have a place to take cover, a last resort against the violent intrusions of angry outsiders itching for any excuse to shoot. It wasn't just a place for storing books. The room represented sanctuary, a shelter and a safe place to hide.

None of which made sense if the lock was on the wrong side.

She looked at her husband. Had a hard time believing this wasn't something he already knew. But she also didn't feel like arguing. And so for want of something else to say, she repeated the statement. "You fucked up my auntie's door."

Then shut it.

She could feel Curtis watching her as she walked across the room and took a seat at Aunt Trudy's dressing table. People were coming over that night and she needed to get ready. She reached into her makeup bag, dipped an acrylic nail into a pot of rouge, and smoothed a shimmery streak of mauve across her cheekbones.

"Looking good tonight," Curtis said.

Dabbed green eye shadow across her lids, smoothed it out with the tip of her finger. Twisted a cap, puckered up, cradled a kiss in dark shining gloss.

"Look good, smell good. Hair all done up . . ."

She glanced back at Curtis.

"Stephanie's coming tonight. You hear me, Curtis?"

"That why you pulling out all the stops? Still trying to impress your sister?"

Lynette shook her head. He drank too much back in Houston too, but that was different—just a little something to take the edge off. Well, maybe not a little. But it was never really a problem before, the way things didn't have to be a problem when it was just the two of them coasting along. When he was still booking gigs and she was still working as a waitress at the *Fleur de Lis*. When everything was pretty much fine.

"Just don't embarrass me tonight," Lynette said.

There was a knock on the bedroom door: "Mama? You in there?"

"What is it?"

"Paula's going to Kenneth's house to watch a movie. Can I go too?"

"No, ma'am."

"But Mama—"

"I can't tell your cousin what to do. But I don't want you running around in the street at night. It's not safe."

Lynette listened to her ten-year-old daughter suck her teeth on the other side of the door, then the sound of feet stomping down the hall. She looked at her husband, the saxophone case lying at his feet.

It was the music that had seduced her, all those years ago. Spoke so powerfully to some craving in her heart that she'd followed the sound of it all the way to Houston. Now he hardly ever played. And who was he really, without the music?

Someone she couldn't trust to carry out a simple task.

She turned away from him and glanced down at a scuff mark on her left shoe. Decided to change into the red pumps.

Behind her back she heard the mattress squeak as Curtis rose to his feet. "Lynette, I want you to know I'm going to make this up to you. . . ."

And Lynette was thinking, *Too late*. Now she was probably going to have to go ahead and get a divorce.

"Because I lied to you, just like you lied to me. . . ."

A divorce: daughter crying, Aunt Trudy wailing. Sister Stephanie shaking her head saying, "I told you so." Man she'd married begging her not to leave him. When she was already gone.

"So now I figure we're even. . . ."

All because of a lock. A lock which now seemed emblematic of all the things she didn't feel like arguing about anymore. Maybe their marriage simply could not withstand the scrutiny of the house. Because every time she looked around all she saw was the sacrifices of the people who had lived there. Not just Uncle Leon but her aunt and her mother—all the people who had come before. People who didn't just give up. When the going got rough they kept going, kept struggling so that their children could have better chances in life. And what had Lynette done with those chances? Squandered them, chasing after some man she'd somehow gotten it in her head was more beautiful than she was. As if she didn't remember, as if it didn't matter. Who she was, where she came from. All the things surrounding a lock her husband had been too high and careless to realize he'd put on the wrong side.

". . . When I told you I didn't open that door."

She looked at Curtis. "What did you just say?"

"You heard me," Curtis said. "We're the ones who robbed that store. That's the real reason Henry sent Paulie to Tampa. Now Paulie's in jail and he's been keeping quiet, but there's no telling how long he'll stay that way."

"What? What are you saying?" Lynette blinked. "Why would you do something so stupid?"

"Why, the money of course. Trying to get us out of your aunt's house, get us our own place. Isn't that what you wanted?"

Lynette stared at her husband. Pitiful, is what it was. And the truly sad part was that, even without the music, she could still see how he might be considered handsome to a girl of, say, nineteen.

Problem was she hadn't been nineteen in ten years.

"What'd you do with the rest of it? The other stuff Paulie took from that store?"

"We got it somewhere safe."

His laces were undone, his pants were unzipped. Fingers plucking at his sleeve.

"Well, now, that's real reassuring, Curtis." Lynette nodded. "How about you tell me where?"

"Well that's the thing I . . ." He cocked his head and squinted.

"Lynette? How'd you know Montgomery was hiding Henry's things in a freezer?"

Lynette opened her mouth to say something then pursed her lips closed again.

"Lynette? You know something you not telling me?"

She tried to turn away from him, but he reached for her arm, spun her back around to face him.

"Lynette? This is not a game. Do you know what Henry will do if he finds out you know something and didn't tell him?"

Lynette watched the glare of headlights sag across his face as a car pulled up to the curb outside.

"That's them." She nodded towards the window. "My sister . . ."

They listened to a door slam, heels click across the pavement, the muffled sound of a man and a woman arguing as they moved up the front walk. The doorbell rang, the chain pulled back, voices wafted up through the walls as Aunt Trudy led Stephanie and her husband through to the safety of inside.

Decent people, Lynette thought and stared into her husband's eyes. *Where I come from, who I am, the way I was raised—*

"Sean told you, didn't he?"

"Why would Sean tell me anything?"

"Why?" Curtis shook his head. "You still think I don't know, don't you?"

He leaned forward, gritted his teeth, and then whispered in her ear: "Why are you getting all dressed up, Lynette? Fixing your hair, changing your clothes . . ."

His voice was a clanging sound, jagged and off-key.

Lynette pulled away from him, held her body back stiffly and stared into his eyes. And even as she felt his grip slacken on her arm, a little voice inside her head was telling her to look at him for once, to really *look*.

"It was Sean, wasn't it?" Curtis said.

He balled his fist while the look in his eyes seemed to ground down into something wild. "You're fucking him, aren't you?"

This man has lost his mind.

Up until that moment she still thought it was the whiskey holding him back, keeping him down.

"It's all right, I forgive you—"

All at once she knew she'd had it wrong. The drinking wasn't holding him down. It was propping him up, keeping him afloat. The whiskey was simply the glue that would not dry.

"You hear me, Lynette? I want to start over."

She tried to break free of his grip and out of instinct, turned towards the closet and a three-foot-high wooden door carved into its back wall.

"I want to start over—"

And only then remembered how much things had changed, how much they themselves had changed them. Because the room she'd been running towards was supposed to represent sanctuary, the need for respite, a safe place to hide.

"You still love me, don't you, baby?"

None of which made sense if the lock was on the wrong side.

The Blinking What.

Stephanie Lawrence, don't do it.

What on earth was she crying for? Sitting on the couch, in the middle of Aunt Trudy's living room, Styrofoam cup in hand. She turned her head, reached under her glasses and stroked her eyelashes with the tip of her finger, trying to preserve the integrity of her mascara. It's sanctity. She hadn't gotten all dressed up and put on makeup just to have it run away from her. In galloping tears.

"Stephanie?"

Except she was laughing too. Jittery, high-pitched squeals roaring up from the pit of her stomach. Loud bursts that made other people in the room cock their heads and stare as they walked past her on their way to the porch. They looked shocked, like they hadn't expected her to make so much noise. It was loud enough to be heard in the parlor where the man who had sent her husband out to the ATM outside the Byrdie's Burgers up the block was still sitting at the folding table, smiling.

"Are you all right?"

She looked at the poor man sitting next to her and good lord he was fine. Just plopped down on the couch next to her and there she was all alone and on her fourth beer. Sean, he'd said his name was. And he just looked so . . . concerned. That was probably why just a moment ago she'd been trying to come up with some discreet way to get her hand around his thigh.

"No, for real, can I get you some water?"

"I'm fine," Stephanie said. She looked back towards the parlor door.

The last time she saw her husband he was sitting in there, playing poker and losing badly. He did that sometimes, when he was really mad, found a way to make a show of wasting great quantities of money because what better way to remind her that ultimately it was still his? The car she drove, the house they lived in: Wasn't he the one who'd actually gone out and earned these things? Which meant her outrage and indignation could only go so far. Yes, they were partners, but if he wanted to plow through their savings, that was his choice, not hers. She'd snagged Prince Charming and it turned out he could be trifling. Which was funny. Or else sad. Anyhow, she was laughing about it.

"You're Stephanie, right? Lynette's sister?"

Something about Sean's voice made a shiver run through her, like a tickle. Just a moment before she had been utterly convinced that the best course of action would be to simply lean forward and tell him so.

"I've heard a lot about you. Been wanting to meet you for a long time . . ."

Drop her hand on his pants leg, squeeze his thigh, and whisper: *I just want to fuck you, is all.* With her eyes closed. She was convinced that that would make her feel better right away.

"Something I need to tell you. Something I'd like you to know . . ."

She wanted to fuck Sean with her eyes closed. And on top this time. Usually lately she just lay on her back, stared up at the ceiling, and counted backwards from one hundred and—

"Sorry for your loss."

She straightened up.

"What?"

"Your uncle. My condolences."

"You knew my uncle?"

"Well, not personally. I knew him like everybody knew him. Enough to know he was a great man."

Stephanie nodded. It was true. They didn't make men like Uncle Leon anymore. Or if they did she'd never been able to get her hands on one. She'd tried too, back in college; had been lied to and cheated on by so many handsome charismatic men that by the time she met her husband it didn't even feel like settling anymore. It felt strategic.

She looked at Sean.

"Excuse me," she said and stood up quickly. Started walking and by the time she realized she didn't know where she was going, she was already swirling through the seamless echo of the crowd. Cup held over her head, thin smile plastered across her lips. Winding and push-ing her way past cousins and friends of friends—contingent relations, a series of obstacles and obligations whose names she couldn't even remember. She stumbled up the stairs, crept inside the bathroom, and locked the door. Leaned against it, breathing hard for a moment, in the dark where it was safe.

A beat was missing. Sean's smile was fading from her now, spinning off into quiet shadows. *What did you almost just do?* It wasn't like her to think that way, to want that way. She was smarter than that.

A beat was missing. *But I don't want to be poor*, Stephanie thought. That was the simple truth of it. What would happen if she actually gave her husband legitimate grounds for divorce? Money was supposed to mean the freedom to do what she wanted. Instead it felt like a trap. She could already see Lynette shaking her head: *I told you. Thought you were so smart and look at you now: all that education and no job. Expensive tastes and no money . . .*

After Lynette ran off to Houston and broke their mama's heart, Stephanie had prided herself for not making the same mistake. One married for love and the other for money and somehow neither one of them was happy. She'd been foolish, she could see that now. Made the mistake of believing in a man more than he believed in himself. That was all Prince Charming really asked of you, wasn't it? That you believe. In fairy tales men were judged by their actions, women by the quality of their belief. While men set out to conquer the world and search for treasure, women spent their lives waiting for some man to come save them. They dropped out of school, gave up on their own ambitions. Signed prenups as testimonials of faith. Created high towers of their own design and then waited for Prince Charming to come unlock the door.

She shut her eyes, breathed a silent prayer for love and patience, and when she was finished, flicked on the light.

That was when she heard the knock.

"Aunt Trudy?" she heard a voice say. It sounded like a little girl on the verge of tears. It startled her, made her hands shake.

"Aunt Trudy?"

The sound of it was not coming from the door but the wall.

"Who's that?"

"It's me. Lynette . . . Who's that?"

"It's Stephanie."

"Oh. Well, thank goodness. You got to get me out of here."

Stephanie shut the medicine cabinet. She reached for the door-knob, stuck her head outside, and peeked down the hall. But she didn't see anything but a blank wall.

"Lynette? There's no door."

"Listen to me, Stephanie. I can tell you've been drinking, so try to focus. I'm locked in the trick room. Remember? In Aunt Trudy's bedroom. We used to play in there when we were kids. Go in there and look in the back of the closet."

"Are you kidding me?"

"You hear me talking to you, don't you? Please, just do it. . . ."

Stephanie stared at her face in the mirror.

"Stephanie? You still there?"

"Yeah. What are you doing locked in a trick room, Lynette?"

Silence.

"It's a reasonable question. Don't you think?"

"Well . . . Curtis and I had a little argument. He didn't want me talking to someone at the party and—"

"Is that what goes on between you two? How you people resolve your differences? He locks you up in trick rooms?"

"Not usually, no . . ."

Silence.

"Stephanie? Don't call me 'you people. . . .'"

Stephanie stared at the mirror while images swirled around her mind like want. Sean sitting next to her on the couch, face flooded with concern. And then, of course, everything she had going for her, her sister had going too. All of a sudden it just made sense.

"It's that guy downstairs, that good-looking one, that Sean." She nodded to her reflection. "You're fucking him, aren't you?"

She heard a kick, strong enough to rattle glass. "Are you going to open the door or what?"

"Hang on."

She walked down the hall, turned a corner, and pushed open the door to Aunt Trudy's room, where she found her niece sprawled across a pink coverlet, staring at the TV on the dresser, watching reruns of *The Cosby Show*. She hadn't been in there in years, but she still remembered coming to visit when she and Lynette were little girls: pawing through Aunt Trudy's jewelry box, dousing themselves with the ancient bottles of cologne that lined her dressing table. Staring at their reflections in a gilded frame mirror while they clutched tubes of grown women's lipstick, twisted the caps, and watched them unfurl like secret scrolls.

She looked back at her niece. Something told her it was probably better not to let the child see her mother climb out of a trick room.

"Why don't you go across the street and play with your friend Kenneth?"

"But Mama said—"

"She told me it's okay."

"For real?"

"Yes. But you have to go now. Your mom will pick you up later. Just stay there until she comes to get you. Understand?"

"Thanks, Aunt Stephanie."

Stephanie watched the girl scramble to her feet and race out of the room. Then she walked to the closet, pulled back the door, and pushed back the curtain of clothes. There it was, just like she remembered: a three-foot-high wooden door. She crouched down and gripped the brass knob. But it was locked.

She walked back to the bathroom. "Lynette? The bolt is locked."

"Well, you got to find the key then," Lynette said. "Figure something out, get me the fuck out of here—"

"Calm down. I'll get Aunt Trudy."

"No! Don't say anything to anyone. I mean it, Stephanie. Get me out of here first. . . ."

Silence.

"He hit me."

"What?"

"You heard me," Lynette said. "It's not a game."

Stephanie stared at her face in the mirror.

"I'll be right back," she said.

She walked back downstairs to the living room where Curtis was still scowling in the corner and Sean was still laughing on the couch. She wound her way past them and down a crowded hall, was just about to push through the swinging door to Aunt Trudy's kitchen when a hand reached out, grabbed her by the forearm, and spun her around.

"Oh, it's you," Stephanie said. She stared at her husband. "So, you got back all right I see. Well, that's good. . . ."

Her husband gave her arm a tight squeeze and pulled her to his chest. He bent down and whispered in her ear: "I think we should leave. Now."

He glanced towards the living room. "How well do you really know these people, anyway?"

"Well enough not to flash a platinum card before I sit down to play a game of poker with them, I imagine."

Her husband smiled. "What's that supposed to mean? I thought it was just a friendly game. This is your family, after all. These are your people—"

"Don't talk to me like that. I told you before—"

"You told me what?"

She looked down at his hand clamped around her arm.

"Never mind," Stephanie said and shook her arm loose. "Why

don't you go outside and wait for me, would you? I just want to tell Aunt Trudy good-bye. If anybody asks why you're leaving, tell them you have to check on your niece. I told her she could play across the street until Lynette got back."

He nodded his head and started walking away from her. She turned and pushed through a swinging door. There in the middle of a bright yellow kitchen, she found Aunt Trudy sitting by herself at a small Formica table.

"Hey, Aunt Trudy," Stephanie said. "What are you doing sitting in here all alone?"

"Still my house, ain't it?" Aunt Trudy scowled. Floral housecoat, wig of glossy auburn curls. Hand wrapped around the handle of a small white teacup as she pursed her lips and peered at Stephanie over the rim. "I can sit wherever I please."

"True enough." Stephanie nodded. She peeked through the kitchen door as her husband slunk back across the shag carpet and Sean and Curtis laughed. A wave of nausea rolled through her stomach as she closed the door behind her and pulled the latch. *Pitiful, is what it is*, she thought. *Like an ache.*

She stared at her aunt. "You seen my sister lately, by any chance?"

"Why?"

"I'm just asking."

"I don't know where that girl is." Aunt Trudy sucked her teeth. "Look at all these crazy people she and that fool dragged into my house. I'm sorry I let them through the front door if you want to know the truth."

"I imagine you are."

"Is that right?" Aunt Trudy squinted at her. "Because you sure seemed to be enjoying yourself well enough. And your man too. I saw him in there, throwing all his money away. What's the matter with him? What's his problem?"

"I don't really know," Stephanie said. She walked across the room, opened the drawer next to the sink, looking for something to open a door.

Aunt Trudy turned her head towards the window as a police siren whizzed past the house. "I guess it don't really matter now," she said. She watched her niece rummage through her silverware drawer, then chuckled when Stephanie turned around holding up a butter knife.

"What you gonna do with that?" Aunt Trudy said. "I said, what you gonna do with that?"

Stephanie looked down at the knife. Her first thought had been that maybe she could wedge it between the door and the wall, pry something open somehow.

Aunt Trudy stared at her. "Ain't got a lot of sense, now, have you?"

"No, ma'am," Stephanie said. "Never said I did."

She put the knife back in the drawer.

"You and your sister both." Aunt Trudy shook her head. "Always been crazy like that. Huh? Ever since you were little girls. And everybody thought you was the one with the smarts, but when you come right down to it, both of you stuck in the same mess.

"Looking for this?" Trudy held up the key to the truck in the shed behind the house.

"No. I need a key. Just not that one."

"Wrong again. This is the key you need. Because they're coming."

"Who?"

"The police. Go on, do like your mother. Get out while you still can."

Stephanie frowned. "Nobody's coming, Aunt Trudy."

"They are though. Gonna raid the place."

"Why would you say that?"

"Because I called them."

"You? Why would you do that?"

"Want my house cleared out. I can't handle all this madness. I couldn't think of any other way to get them out of my house."

Stephanie nodded. It occurred to her that her aunt might have been scared of Curtis and his friends and not known how to admit it.

Another siren whizzed past the house.

"You should have asked for help."

"Who? I'm an old woman, girl. Been alone for fifteen years. Had my work, my friends. Can't none of them help me now. There wasn't nobody else."

"There was me," Stephanie said. "You should have called me."

Stephanie turned back around, still looking for some way to get a door open.

"You? What are you going to do?" Aunt Trudy asked. She watched her niece paw around the cabinet next to the refrigerator. She shook her head.

"All this trouble going on, world falling apart all around you. And you just stand there blinking—"

"What? No, I'm listening, Aunt Trudy." Stephanie wheeled around, clutching an ice pick.

Aunt Trudy stared at her. "But you not *hearing*," she said.

There was a loud knock at the front door.

"Listening and hearing is two different things," Aunt Trudy said. "Just like looking and seeing."

Stephanie looked at the ice pick. What did she know about picking a lock? She put the pick down and looked around the room again. She walked over to the door that led to the backyard, turned the knob, and stuck her head outside.

"You see I *saw* that fool Lynette brought here," Aunt Trudy said. "Just like I hear everything that goes on in my house. And that's why . . . But what about you? What about that one you got? You think my husband ever gambled? How's your man any better, when push comes to shove?" She shook her head and chuckled. "Y'all sure know how to pick 'em, don't you?"

"Can't argue with you on that," Stephanie said. She stared across the weeded hill of Aunt Trudy's backyard, to the small toolshed leaning against the fence. When she opened the door she could see the getaway truck under a blue tarp. "But there's not a lot I can do about that right now."

"You could sit and talk to me for a minute," Aunt Trudy said. "Quit all that bopping around. . . ."

There was another loud knock on the front door, then the sound of footsteps scrambling around the living room. A woman screamed, and a few seconds later a man cried out, *Don't do it! Wait!*

Aunt Trudy stood up. Put her hand on her hip, cocked her head out the back door, and stared at her niece digging through her toolshed.

"I'm trying to *help* you, girl," she called to Stephanie. "Can't you see that? Teach you something about life—"

"Some other time, Aunt Trudy," Stephanie said. She turned around and walked back into the kitchen, fists wrapped tight around the handle of a sledgehammer.

"I want to talk, I really do. But first I gotta go open a door."

Five People
Who Crave Sauce

(1999)

1.

Ever since she was a little girl Desiree poured ketchup on her ham and eggs and sausage and hash browns and pork chops and hot dogs and hamburgers and meatloaf and tuna melts and chicken fingers and catfish and corn fritters and onion rings and come to think of it anything fried. They were all missing something and somehow that sweet and savory, tart and tangy taste almost always did the trick. Throughout her childhood she'd stared down at the plates set before her then up into the eyes of the various loved ones who'd prepared her meals and thought to herself, *No offense but this needs ketchup*.

Then, one night when she was older, left to her own devices and really, really broke, she found herself standing alone in the kitchen of the tiny apartment she shared with her husband, Craig. She opened the refrigerator and stood blinking at the harsh light that flashed above empty white shelving units stained with soy sauce, coffee grounds, and the hard, cracked edge of what once had been a perfectly edible wedge of cheese. *Hungry*, she thought and grabbed a bottle of ketchup.

She squirted it onto a plate. *Last lick*, she thought. Was there anything more satisfying than a last lick? The way when she was finished eating she always scooped what was left onto her finger and put it into her mouth because she wanted that to be the taste that stayed with her when she stood up from the table. She grabbed a fork, walked into the living room, and clicked on the TV. Then sat on the couch sucking on metal prongs and waiting to feel full.

After a while she couldn't help but realize that something was missing, that what she had smeared across her plate was not, technically, food. She put down her fork and looked around her empty apartment. Ketchup was perfect, yes, but the word she was looking for was compliment.

Such was the nature of sauce. It was an enhancer, a taste-bringer-outer. Even the most delicious and universally admired wanted in its essence to be a part of something larger than itself. It craved merger, could only truly be itself or realize its full potential in the presence of the other—no matter how indistinct or ultimately bland that other was.

She stared at the TV and waited for her husband to come home.

At some point during the next four hours it occurred to Desiree that she could always pour it into a bowl and add water, heat it up and call it soup. But that seemed like unnecessary subterfuge at that point.

She picked up her fork, dipped it back into her plate of ketchup. And that was what she had for dinner.

2.

Hot sauce, on the other hand, was a legitimate fetish and Craig slathered it on everything to the point of pain. He sat at the end of the crowded bar, reached into his jacket pocket, and twisted the cap off a small glass vial he had purchased from the back of a truck the last time he went to visit his mama in Louisiana.

"Never leave home without it." Craig winked to the man sitting next to him—his former supervisor, Todd. He held the bottle out like an assertion of his identity, as in, "That's just how we do it where I come from." Hot was how he was raised and how he liked it. Hot was how it had to be, or else he swore it had no taste at all.

He watched the waitress lower his plate on the counter, the smell of pork loins, okra, and spicy greens strong enough to make him swoon. He thanked Todd for the meal. Next time, Craig said, it was on him.

"Don't worry about it." Todd smiled. "After all you've been through, it's the least I can do. I hope you know how sorry I am to have to let you go. Things just didn't work out the way I'd hoped."

Craig nodded and said nothing. He shook the bottle and sprinkled red tangy spurts over his plate.

Todd looked around the bar. "Where's Desiree?"

"Oh, she couldn't make it." Craig shrugged. His hands were shaking. "We had a little falling-out."

"Nothing serious, I hope?"

"Oh, no, nothing like that. Just a little falling-out. We'll be all right." He shook the bottle. The stress of trying to smile like he was more grateful than hungry caused him to lose his concentration. Hot sauce splattered over his meat, two vegetable sides, and piece of cornbread.

"I hope so. That's a good woman you got there, Craig. I know it's been hard lately. But you two just hang tough. You got skills, man. You'll find another job."

"Yes, sir," Craig said.

Todd set an envelope on the bar. Then he stood up and patted Craig on the shoulder. As he walked away Craig opened up the envelope and counted the money inside. His severance pay: the last money he could expect to see any time in the near future. When he finished counting, Craig tucked the envelope in the pocket of his jacket, twisted the cap back on his bottle of hot sauce, and set it down on the counter.

He picked up his fork, poked and swirled around the dark mysteries of his plate. He scooped up something heavy and thick and popped it into his mouth. His eyes rolled up to the back of his head as he swallowed, and no one watching could tell if it was agony or ecstasy that made him moan—although when asked he always swore it was the latter.

"That's just how I was raised," Craig gasped. All taste subsumed by heat. It was a tongue number, a desensitizer, and although Craig never thought about it, probably why he always needed more.

He finished his meal, scraping his plate with the side of his fork. He swallowed his last bite of food. He ordered a drink. Then another, then another. He spun around on his stool, watched the room spin around him in hot wheezing laughter, sharp voices that whirled and coughed and swooned. For a moment he felt nauseous and clutched his drink for balance until the churning heat in his stomach subsided, leaving a prickly aftertaste, vinegary and strangely sweet.

Like her, Craig thought. His wife, Desiree, so sticky and sweet, no doubt at that moment sitting on the couch, waiting for him to come home. A quick image of his tongue batting against the tears falling from her eyes flashed through Craig's mind. That was what salt tasted like: even her smiles bothered and begged for things. When he couldn't swallow her want. He had enough trouble keeping down his own.

"I'll go home when I'm good and ready," he said to no one in particular. "And anyway I'm enjoying my fucking self." He reached inside the envelope, slammed a twenty on the counter, and ordered another drink.

After a while he realized that what he needed was a physical sensation as real as hunger, something to make his eyes water, his palms sweat, purge his sinuses of senseless clutter.

I know, Craig thought. He looked around until he saw a tall, skinny woman flirting with the bartender. He stood up and asked if she wanted to come sit on his lap.

3.

Millie jiggled and swished on high heels as she followed Craig out to the parking lot, a belly full of ramen noodles sloshing around in her stomach. The instructions on the bag said to add a cup of water but she always added two, supplementing the watery sauce from the flavor packet with a hefty dash of Lawry's Seasoned Salt.

She climbed into the back seat of Craig's car. She had already blotted out most of her childhood like a bad dream, but every time she had cause to move her arm in a quick up-and-down motion she found herself assaulted by private visions of the fat jiggling on her mother's forearms as she shook a bottle of Lawry's into her famous potato salad. Wasn't a thing in this world that couldn't use a little Lawry's, her mother always said. You just twist the cap, shake it out, and soon enough you'd see what she meant.

Soon enough, Millie thought and shut her eyes. Craig's kisses were full of vinegar and cigarette ash, and when she slipped her hand into his pants, his penis was surprisingly small. She crouched down and put her finger in his mouth. Craig tasted something searing and salty merging with the saliva in his throat, bringing to life a tangy aftertaste of heat. It broke apart into peppers and pungent oils and for one brief moment all his thoughts were perfectly clear. He sucked on her fingers still coated in MSG. Delicious and satisfying was what it was.

Millie put her head down. Sometimes when she squinted in the dark she'd start seeing her mama standing over her, stirring her bowl, great globs of potato salad clinging to her spoon as she raised it to her mouth, where it stuck to the bottom of her chin. Regardless of whatever else she was doing her mind would start wandering towards smooth, rich, creamy, thick-as-oblivion mayonnaise and all the fat that during daylight she liked to tell herself she'd left behind years ago.

When they were finished Millie climbed out of the car. Craig zipped up his pants and reached into the envelope stuffed in his pocket. He handed her a fifty-dollar bill.

"Take care of yourself," Craig said, and Millie smiled, vaguely aware that she needed to pee.

She whipped her head around and headed up the block still smiling, even as her eyes sank and settled into something solid and fixed. Her night vision: walking in the middle of the street while her eyes scanned the sidewalk and alleyways and garbage cans and places where hungry things liked to hide. All the while she could feel something bubbling up in her stomach—onion, vinegar, semen, pepper, whiskey, and vodka—churning around the noodles. She stopped walking and inhaled deeply, put a hand to her heartbeat, and waited for the feeling to roll back like the tide.

She stood up, took another deep breath, and started walking again. She'd made it all the way to the Byrdie's Burgers on the corner of Seventh Avenue when a man's voice called out from the shadows.

"Cocoa? Is that you?"

"For fuck's sake," Millie said. "Not now. Not again."

The man was already walking towards her. There she was, half-sick, stuff bubbling up in her throat, mind pitching and rolling, Mama still sucking on that wooden spoon in her mind. She was out there starving, just trying to hold on, to keep it together long enough to get back home, and on top of all of that having to pee.

"Cocoa? It's me, Gerard. . . ."

"Dammit," Millie said. She reached down and unsnapped her purse, started digging around through the dust and Doublemint wrappers and Quickie Mart receipts trying to find something as hard and sharp as hunger.

"Cocoa?"

She'd been through this before.

4.

Chocolate brown, Gerard thought. Standing on the corner, draped in golden robes of shadows, shaking her head and reaching into her purse. Ruby-red lips soft and sweet as cherry syrup—*my chocolate sauce, my sweetness, my yummy brown queen*. It was Cocoa all right. Gerard would know her anywhere.

"Cocoa? Is that you?"

She didn't answer. Nerves, that's all it was. It had been such a long time since they'd seen each other; he could feel it too, like hunger. And the truth was he'd been hungry for a long time. Even before he lost his bed at the shelter, before his sister kicked him out, before they tore down his daddy's grocery store to make room for the highway. In some ways his whole life was a map of a hunger that he'd been set to wander the day she told him good-bye.

"Cocoa? It's me, Gerard. . . ."

He stepped towards her. What were they even arguing about? What childish thing had made him turn his back on her all those years ago? Refuse to answer her call? He couldn't even remember. All he knew was he'd been hungry ever since. Nothing tasted the same after she left him, and then he couldn't taste at all. He could eat and drink all he wanted, flood his mind trying to drown out the hunger in his heart, but he was never satisfied. Because all he really wanted was her. He clutched his empty stomach, licked his lips, and stepped towards her, arms stretched wide for her to climb inside. Hungry.

"Cocoa?"

"I told you before, old man," Millie said. When he took another step towards her she stabbed the back of his left hand with a nail file.

"I'm not your damn Cocoa."

Gerard stared down at his damaged hand. Then up at the woman jogging away from him towards the bus stop on the corner, still gripping her nail file. After a while he could see it: the difference, the distance . . . Not what he wanted at all.

He called out, "I'm sorry, miss. I thought you were someone else—"

The crosstown bus pulled up and Millie counted out one, two, three bags of ramen noodles and then dumped a whole handful of quarters into the slot. She took her seat and stared out the window, watched Gerard walk away from the curb then settle back into the shadows, one hand clutching his empty stomach, the other raised to his mouth to lick his own wounds.

She rode the bus all the way across town. She walked to her apartment and unlocked the front door.

"Mimi?"

She put a crumpled fifty-dollar bill in a jar on the kitchen table.

"Mimi . . . ?"

5.

She found her grandmother in the living room, sitting in the easy chair with the TV on, a blanket wrapped around her shoulders and a smile on her face, eyes closed and dreaming of the perfect roux.

The Last Suspicious Holdout

(2001)

The entire facility reeked of garlic, and at first Claudette couldn't tell
where the smell was coming from. Just a noxious odor she noticed
as soon as she entered the building that then followed her down a
narrow corridor, up a short flight of stairs, and into the main office of
the Leon Moore Center for Creative Unity. It wasn't overwhelming,
just strong enough to be noticeable, contributing to a more general
sense of unease as she presented herself to the heavyset woman in
the peach-colored blouse seated behind the front desk. Although it
also occurred to Claudette that perhaps her sensitivity to it was just
another side effect of the hormones.

The woman at the desk was talking on the phone when Claudette
entered, but she smiled and raised a long, manicured finger to indicate
she'd be with her in a moment. Claudette looked around the office,
an attempt to get her bearings, but she was also still searching for the
source of the odd scent. It was a box-shaped room with high ceilings, yellow walls, and faded green carpeting. To her left was a worn
tan couch and brown coffee table, on which sat a stack of brochures.
Next to the couch was a small wooden bookcase filled with used pa-
perbacks. Above the bookcase was a large framed photograph of a
group of enthusiastic young people standing on a bridge in matching
T-shirts and bell-bottom pants. They were all holding shovels, smiling

beneath a large banner that hung from the bridge's rafters that read "Empowering the People Through Creative Unity." To her right was a set of metal doors.

When the woman hung up the phone Claudette stated her name and asked to speak to the assistant director. In response the woman smiled, stood, and introduced herself as Millicent Jones.

"Welcome!"

"Pleasure to meet you," Claudette said and extended her hand.

"Wow, look at you!" Millicent said. She seized Claudette's hand and shook it vigorously, long fingernails digging into Claudette's skin. "I mean, we've been expecting you. And now here you are!"

"Well, let me start by saying what a pleasure it is to have this opportunity to visit the Center in person," Claudette said. "We at Byrdie Bird's Family of Friends appreciate the contributions your organization has made to your community over the years and are proud to have been able to support those efforts for as long as we have been."

The shaking stopped.

"Have been?"

A phone beeped. Claudette felt the vibration in the left interior pocket of her blazer and removed her palm from Millicent's grip.

"Excuse me," she said and pulled out her cell phone. A message from her husband flashed on the screen, reminding her that she had a doctor's appointment at 4:15. She pressed a button and tucked her cell back into her pocket.

When she looked up again, Millicent was frowning.

"Sorry," she said. "What?"

"You said 'have been,'" Millicent said. "Just now, you used the past tense, when describing Byrdie's support. I couldn't help but notice that. There's not a problem, is there?"

"Not at all."

"You can tell me the truth."

"I wouldn't call it a problem, Millicent, so much as a complication. One that ultimately has little to do with you. You see, normally it is our policy at Byrdie Bird's to make biannual visits to each of the initiatives we sponsor. Somehow your organization was bypassed during the past few rotations." She smiled. "Everything will get sorted out, don't worry. Really, I'm just here to help."

This was not true and, from the expression on Millicent's face, it was clear that both women realized this. Officially, Claudette was an internal auditor with Byrdie Bird's Family of Friends, the charitable division of Byrdie's Burgers Food Corporation, an international fast-food chain which, for reasons not entirely clear, had been providing a significant portion of the Center's budget for the past fifteen years. Her primary responsibilities involved oversight—making sure the money went where it was supposed to go and then that it was being used properly—but, because of the ways the work of her division intersected Byrdie's Burgers' overall public profile, her actual job was often more complicated. The success or failure of a given initiative could not be assessed in strictly financial terms and, on the one hand, there was the sincere desire to ensure that the initiatives they sponsored genuinely contributed to the public good while, on the other (larger, stronger) hand, there was the real need to ensure that none of them did anything that might reflect negatively on the Byrdie's Burgers brand. A digital monitoring system had been set up to track coverage across media and any explicit, negative reference to the division was immediately flagged. While this was helpful for identifying potential problems, it couldn't always be counted on to pinpoint their source. Which was where Claudette came in. She was, when necessary and regardless of her official title, the boots on the ground.

"It's the vandalism, isn't it?" Millicent said. "The real reason you're here? Because I hope you realize we had nothing to do with that. As hard as we work trying to build this community up? How could anyone think we'd turn around and tear it down? The very idea is insulting and everyone knows it, including that half-wit Edward Stone."

Millicent was referring to a recent broadcast on a local radio station during which a newscaster named Edward P. Stone had gone on
a twenty-minute rant about the current lawlessness in his hometown.
It seemed the locals were being terrorized by an as-yet unidentified
vandal who'd spent the past few weeks spray-painting the name of
the Center all over town. The words "Moore Creative Unity" could
now be seen spelled out in jagged print on the walls and windows of
several north side businesses and private residences, including three
Byrdie's Burgers franchises. Although it was the tagging of a parked
police cruiser that had precipitated Stone's outburst, in the process of
venting his rage he'd mentioned the fact that Byrdie's Burgers was the
primary sponsor of the Center itself, using this fact to make a vague
argument about biting the hand that feeds.

"Trust me, Millicent. It's not about the vandalism," Claudette
said, although, in one sense, it was entirely about the vandalism. That
was the reason the Center had been flagged. But the real problem
was the chain of events the flagging had triggered within the division
itself. No one was certain where Mr. Stone had gotten his information because it seemed no one currently employed at the company
was aware of it. An internal investigation had uncovered an isolated
contribution to the Center back in 1985, which had been improperly
recorded and, as a result, replicated annually. According to the current version of events, the mistake had somehow gone unnoticed and
therefore uncorrected for more than fifteen years.

"Good," Millicent said. "Forgive me for being so blunt, but this
situation really caught me off guard. First, we got Stone spewing his
nonsense and then I find out you're coming. Nobody told me about
your visit until yesterday, which means I didn't really have a chance
to prepare. . . ."

Millicent smiled. "Truth? I have to say I felt a little better when I
saw it was you they sent. Although I do realize that, given the current

state of things, it probably either means something very good or very bad. . . ."

Millicent laughed at the comment without bothering explaining it, and in truth she didn't need to. Claudette knew what she meant, although, in this instance, she considered it to mean very little one way or the other. She was a professional and she was there to do a job.

"Rest assured. It's not the vandalism I'm concerned about."

Claudette could feel Millicent watching her closely, trying to intuit meaning from the expression on her face. So she held her face very carefully, not wanting to give anything away. The truth was the situation represented an appalling error of oversight, one that threatened to do real damage to the division's reputation. It was the kind of mistake that cost people their jobs and, in Claudette's opinion, deservedly so. Knowledge of it was at that point confined to a few people within the division and she'd been asked to come to the Center in order to determine the best course of action to mitigate the potential fallout should the error become wider known. She'd agreed to do this even though she was not convinced that the explanation she'd been given was entirely credible. She'd worked in the division for seven years and felt confident she knew her coworkers. They were all, like her, consummate professionals, making it difficult to see how a mistake of this magnitude could have gone unnoticed for as long as it had.

Unless one of them had been actively working to cover it up.

Which meant it was suspicious.

"That's a relief to hear," Millicent said. "Because, I'm telling you, this community is really in crisis right now. I'm not sure if people realize how deeply budget cuts at the federal level have impacted local communities. But, if anything, our presence and your support are now more important than ever."

Claudette nodded. Millicent smiled.

"Why don't I show you around," Millicent said.

"Great!"

She led Claudette through the metal doors. They opened into a dining hall with a red-tiled floor. The room contained seven rows of long tables arranged perpendicular to an open kitchen, and at which a dozen people sat quietly eating. The cooking area was separated from the main space of the room by another long table on which sat a bowl of fruit, a platter of sandwiches wrapped in cellophane, and three large thermoses marked "juice," "milk," and "water." Behind it, a woman in a white apron and auburn wig stood next to a stove, stirring a pot. Stretched across the wall behind her was a banner that read "Creative Unity Nourishes the People."

"That's Mrs. Brown, she's in charge of food service," Millicent said. "We open our doors every morning at six thirty and offer breakfast at no charge, although we do accept donations. We keep serving until ten a.m. or until we run out, whichever comes first. Got a lot of people coming in, and it's not just who you call the indigent. A lot of elderly, a lot of kids on their way to school. Food vulnerability is a real issue for a lot of people around here, and anyone who needs it is welcome."

Claudette nodded and looked at a white bucket in the corner, beneath a large water stain on the ceiling. From where she stood she could identify five health code violations including the jaunty angle of the hairnet on Mrs. Brown's wig. There was also the persistent presence of the strange fumes, which she had at that point accepted were pervasive. In the dining hall the odor was offset by the aroma of citrus and pepper billowing up from the steam rising from whatever Mrs. Brown was cooking. But these new scents mixed and mingled with the garlic smell in such a way that made Claudette doubt the pot constituted its actual source.

"Now Mrs. Brown is a full-time employee, one of seven including me. Otherwise we are sustained entirely through the efforts of volunteers. Fortunately, we have a lot of those. You'd be surprised how many people want to help, want to do something but don't always know how. So that's one thing the Center does—provide an outlet and framework for people who want to lend a hand."

They walked the length of the room then pushed through another set of doors and entered the main space of the Center. It was a large, open room with brick walls, high ceilings, and a cement floor that appeared to have been arranged into distinct quadrants of activity. In one corner a group of children danced on rubber mats while two women clapped and cheered them on. In another, a circle of older men sat on folding chairs whittling small objects they held up to their mouths that appeared to be whistles. Yet another area had been set up like a classroom where a woman stood next to a chalkboard placed in front of three rows of people busy scribbling in notebooks as they sat in small desk chairs. In the middle of the room were two rows of long tables, at which a few people were busy reading and talking among themselves. A stage had been set up along the back wall and a group of five women, bodies draped in bright blue shawls, were standing with their arms raised above them, apparently in the process of rehearsing some sort of performance. Towering above the entire room was a large banner that read "Creative Unity Believes in Self-Defense."

"This is where most of our programming takes place," Millicent said. "Broadly speaking, there are two main divisions, organized into specific units of activity that vary depending on the day and time. We offer seminars on applying for housing grants, basic job skills, mediating social services, negotiating law enforcement, home economics, transcendental meditation, and basic wood working"—she nodded to the circle of men with the carving knives—"all of which falls under basic literacy. Then we have our cultural programming, which includes our history seminars, the speaker's program, the book, debate, poetry, and theatre clubs. In addition, there are a number of outside groups that come in and use the space to hold various meetings."

Claudette stared wordlessly at the jumble of activity taking place before her. Following the initial contribution, the work of the Center had not been tracked and she'd arrived not entirely certain what it was they did there. It was disconcerting to realize how little actually being in the space did to clarify. Children doing calisthenics in one corner, a group of old men whittling in another, while one woman wrote on a chalkboard and another group of women danced on a stage did little to convey any clear sense of intent. It constituted a sharp contrast with the other initiatives her division sponsored—375 well-organized, well-funded facilities that made up the official members of Byrdie Bird's Family of Friends. Testaments to the Byrdie's Burgers ethos, decorative feathers in the hard plastic cap of the Byrdie's Burgers brand. Carefully curated initiatives organized around the franchise model and meant to convey a reassuring sense of professionalism, organization, and, above all, unity of intent.

"You seem to be wearing a lot of hats here," Claudette said. "What would you say was the Center's top priority?"

"Hard to say," Millicent confessed. "In general, we just try to stay true to the original mandate, to be responsive to the needs of the community as opposed to dictating those needs. A lot of ways that can work out."

Claudette nodded. She looked at another banner hanging on the wall above two men seated at one of the long tables, conferring with one another as they stared at a binder open between them. The banner read "Why Not Join the Struggle You Are Already In?" She knew the original donation to the Center predated the adoption of the franchise model, during the brief period in the early 1980s when one of the division's functions had been to demonstrate support for social justice efforts, which were, at the time, taking place in many of the communities they served. Byrdie's Burgers had wanted to be recognized as an integral part of those communities, to remind the public of the significance of the fact that they had remained in inner cities even after most other franchises fled. There'd been an aggressive advertising campaign promoting how Byrdie's provided jobs in areas with high unemployment while continuing to offer hot meals at affordable prices. They sponsored educational scholarships and management training programs designed to help industrious employees to realize the dream of someday becoming owner/operators of franchises of their own. They trumpeted donations to the NAACP and the United Negro College Fund and, in several markets, made small donations to local community groups like the Moore Center. Most of these efforts had been phased out after only a few years, during a period known internally as "the great purge." Research had determined that none of these programs actually made a bit of difference one way or another. People would continue to eat at Byrdie's Burgers regardless.

"Everybody talks about drugs," Millicent said, "and yes, it's a big problem here, same as everywhere else. But underneath all that is the need to address the sources of despair that can lead to crippling addictions themselves. A lack of opportunities, the lack of infrastructural support. The fact that there are so few jobs in our community that pay above minimum wage. Sometimes people find themselves in situations where they can't see any way out and seek escape in the only places they know to look." She shook her head. "A lot of people don't make it back out. Or else they wind up in jail. Because that's what they do now. They throw you in jail. . . ."

Claudette nodded. Whatever they were doing there, Claudette knew they were doing it on a very tight budget. While Byrdie's contribution represented a significant portion of the Center's budget, it was, in truth, just a fraction of the sums received by the other initiatives her division sponsored—official members of the Byrdie Bird's Family of Friends. This fact lent some credibility to the idea that the continued sponsorship was the result of a clerical error. According to the official story, the contributions had gone unnoticed for so long because they represented such an insignificant amount—relatively unimportant right up until the moment Mr. Stone opened his mouth and the Center was flagged.

"Oh, for goodness' sakes," Millicent said and crouched down. A child's drawing lay on the floor. Millicent picked it up and held it out to Claudette. It was a crayon picture of a green monster glowering behind a group of children who stood together, holding hands. Underneath the picture, the words "WE NEED MOORE CREATIVE UNITY" had been written in childish scrawl.

Millicent smiled at the picture. "Kids." She chuckled. "Precious, aren't they? You have any?"

"No. Not yet."

"Me neither," Millicent said. "I guess it's not in the cards for everyone."

She led Claudette across the room, to the children on the mats. Upon closer inspection, Claudette realized they were all barefoot and had whistles hanging from colored yarn draped around their necks. Most of them were laughing and jumping happily, save for one boy near the wall, who sat on the lap of a morose-looking woman with slicked back hair. The boy was crying while the woman stared straight ahead and bounced him on the knee.

Millicent handed the picture to the boy and, as soon as he saw it, the crying stopped.

"I thought this was you." Millicent smiled.

The boy wiped his eyes and stared, transfixed by his own artwork.

"This is our daycare program," Millicent explained. "Right now, we can only accommodate fifteen children, but we're hoping to expand as soon as we're able because, of course, the waiting list is twice as long. . . ."

She turned to the glum-looking woman holding the boy.

"How'd that interview go, Latonya?"

"It went."

Millicent nodded and glanced back at Claudette.

"We'll talk about it later," she said and started walking again, Claudette trailing after her.

"Did you know that a drug felony conviction gets you a lifetime ban from food stamps?" Millicent asked her. "They say it's a deterrent because it's the drugs that are breaking up families but all it really does is penalize women for having a drug felon in the home. But see, then they turn around and penalize you again for being a single mother. They put term limits on benefits because they want women to go back to work. So now we have all these children running around unsupervised while their mommas are working and trying to feed them, and what do they do? Cut funding for after-school programs." She shook her head. "It's crazy, I'm telling you. Honestly? Even I had no idea how crazy until I started working here. . . ."

They passed by another banner that read "Know Your Rights So You Are Prepared to Fight for Them," then stopped when they reached the two men at the table studying the binder.

"Now, that's Attorney Jenkins, he's one of several volunteers who have committed themselves to coming in on a regular basis," Millicent said. "Every week he spends a few hours here, giving legal advice. Can't actually make appearances in court—which is a perfect example of what I've been talking about. He was disbarred due to a possession charge."

Claudette stopped walking.

"Are you saying he's been convicted of a felony?"

"Yes. It's part of what I'm talking about."

Claudette looked back at the group of children. Byrdie Bird's had a very strict policy about employing felons and she knew that the close proximity between a convicted drug felon and an informal daycare was, in and of itself, the potential source of a scandal, serious enough to justify shutting the Center down. Children, after all, were Byrdie's Burgers' core market across all demographics, and anything that called into question the integrity of that relationship was a threat to the company's profile as a whole. Mr. Jenkins may have been harmless, may have had nothing but the best of intentions. But by simply being there, he constituted a threat.

"Did you know that possession of crack or heroin in any amount technically constitutes a felony?" Millicent asked her. "That's right. There are people serving mandatory sentences of twenty years or more just for having an ounce of crack cocaine, regardless of any intent to sell. They'll throw you in jail, make you stay there for as long as they feel like it. And then, when you do get out, even if you did somehow manage to get clean, you're right back in the same situation you were in before. Except now you're saddled with a felony conviction and have to live with that for the rest of your life. Makes it even harder to find a job, to say nothing of the additional pressure it puts on women, trying to cope and care for these children alone."

They kept walking, past the stage where the women were still performing their strange dance. One stood to the side, watching the others, and seemed to be directing their movements. On the wall next to her was a small sign that said simply "Black Is Beautiful."

"That is Shay Williams, she's in charge of our cultural division. She was an EMT for thirty-five years and is also a very accomplished poet. . . . Shay, say hello."

Shay looked at Claudette. "Hello," she said, then turned around and went back to her rehearsal.

"You should also meet Rev Ralston. He works in the literacy program. He's somewhere around here," Millicent said. "Maybe you've heard of him? He was in a very successful jazz trio back in the day, then started working here after he retired."

Claudette shook her head. The name sounded familiar but at first she couldn't place it.

Then it came back.

"Rev Ralston? From the Langston Trio?" Claudette's parents had been fans of the Trio and she'd listened to their music many times as a child. "Rev Ralston works here?"

"He's been affiliated with the Center from the beginning." Millicent smiled. "A close friend of Leon Moore himself."

They reached the opposite side of the room and another door.

"And of course, this is how it all began. . . ."

She pressed her hip against the door and it popped open, unleashing a strong blast of outdoor light.

"I mean that literally. This is our launch pad. . . ."

Claudette followed her outside and found herself standing at the edge of an enormous garden. It was at least twice the size of the Center itself and stretched the entire length of the block. Long rows of citrus trees lined the periphery while the center space was arranged in square plots of vegetables, intersected by gravel walking paths. A group of young men and women picked satsumas, tangerines, and limes; others sat on benches or kneeled in the dirt with hoes, shovels, and wide straw hats.

"I don't know how familiar you are with our history but—"

"I remember." Claudette smiled. She realized Millicent was staring and explained, "I'm from here, actually. Lived on Broad Street until I was nine and my parents moved to the capital."

"Ahhh," Millicent said. She looked relieved. "So you know, then. . . ."

Claudette did know. The Center was located on the corner of what once had been an entire block of burned-out houses, casualties of the disruption and chaos caused by a years-long highway construction project instigated by the city. They'd been a dangerous, ugly eyesore for years until one day Leon Moore and a group of his friends decided to deal with it themselves. They'd gone in with trash bags, jackhammers, and shovels and set about cleaning it all out. They knocked down walls and built new ones, broke up the concrete, and, in the soil underneath, started planting seeds. Over the course of the next two years they'd reimagined the space as a beautiful community garden. Somehow, no one seemed to notice what they were doing until after they'd already done it, at which point the city got involved to remind them that the land, in truth, belonged to someone else. And that was how a movement had begun—as a dispute over the law of adverse possession.

"That's why the Center is so important to people, why the name 'Leon Moore' is so respected. Ultimately, Creative Unity is all about preserving the garden, which, it should go without saying, means preserving the people who created it," Millicent said. "That's why Stone's accusations and lies have got so many people upset around here. Everybody knows we would never support vandalism. In fact, we have done everything we could think of to make it stop. It's why we submitted that proposal to have the street name officially changed."

"Yes, your proposal," Claudette said. She'd read about this in the file she'd been given about the Center before she arrived, which she'd put aside because it had given her a headache. Somehow, in the midst of everything else going on, the Center had decided the time was right to draw even more attention to itself by submitting a proposal to the city council to have the street on which they were located renamed in Leon Moore's honor.

"Remind me where things stand on that?"

"It's in committee. Been in committee for months now. They haven't even voted on it yet."

Claudette nodded. "And then the vandalism started after that?"

Millicent stopped walking. "No. That's not right."

She looked hurt for some reason. "That's not right at all. The vandalism has been going on for almost a year now. It's just nobody paid attention to it until it started showing up on the north side. We submitted our proposal in response to it, thinking that maybe, if we could give people a better way to honor Leon Moore's memory, it would stop. And this is why Mr. Stone's words are dangerous, because, of course, we do realize the timeline is important. And he's creating a situation where we got a lot of people mistaking cause for effect. Even you, apparently. Which I don't really understand because I explained all this to Lena the last time we spoke."

"I'm sure you did," Claudette said. She noticed Millicent called her supervisor "Lena."

"It's in the report, I'm sure. I just wanted to hear from you directly, make sure I have all the facts."

Claudette's cell was beeping again. This time it was her supervisor.

"Speaking of Lena . . ." She held up the phone. "I should take this."

"Of course. Take all the time you need. . . ."

Claudette wandered a few steps away from Millicent, took a seat on a nearby bench, and then pressed a button.

"Have you arrived yet?" Lena asked.

"Yes. I'm here now. The assistant director just gave me the tour."

"And may I ask about your initial impressions?"

"Honestly, Lena?" She looked at a woman in a large straw hat crouched down in front of her, shaping a mound of dirt around a young stalk. "It's fucked. I really don't know what else to say about it. I counted at least five health code violations in the dining hall alone. But more specifically, they have convicted felons working not one hundred feet from what I have no doubt is a completely unlicensed daycare."

"Doing what?"

"I have no idea. But that's just what I've seen so far, and I've only been here an hour."

She shook her head. "I have a hard time understanding how something like this ever happened, much less was allowed to go on for as long as it has."

"Well, that's not what's important right now, is it? We just have to find a way to deal with it. Is integration still a possibility?"

"That would be nice, wouldn't it?"

Claudette watched two barefoot women in blue robes walk towards her on the gravel path, each of them carrying a large wicker basket. The women bowed their heads three times and then made a quick ritualistic gesture with their hands before disappearing through the door.

"Unfortunately, I don't see how that's possible. Even without the felons. My sense is that the situation is already too complicated by the focus on Leon Moore's name."

"The name is not what's important."

"I think it is. To them."

She looked up and saw a man sitting on the bench across from her, peeling an orange.

"These people are pretty eccentric, Lena. We need their approval for something like that, and my impression is that they could easily refuse. It's happened before. And that, in itself, could start a potential brush fire."

"Well, in my experience the best way to put out a fire is to throw money on it," Lena said.

Claudette watched the man across from her drop his orange peels into a small wooden bowl he was holding on his lap. He was wearing blue jeans and a faded cotton shirt and had what looked like home-made shoes made from rubber tires strapped to his feet.

"I'm sorry I had to ask you to do this," Lena said. "Sorry I couldn't just go down there and deal with it myself. But I think we both realize that my leaving the office and dropping everything would have just drawn more attention to the situation. There is always the consideration that our effort to solve a problem does not become the problem itself."

"I suppose. Although it's pretty clear that you've already been down here."

Claudette pivoted her body, lowered her head, and switched the phone to her other ear. "She called you 'Lena.'"

"Who? Millicent?"

Claudette bit her lip and looked past the trees to the other side of the fence that lined the garden, where a man stood alone on the basketball court of the neighboring community center. He was holding a ball and as he dribbled it, a gold necklace that spelled the name "Tony" flipped onto his collarbone.

"Claudette? I want you to do whatever you think is best. You know you have my full authority."

"I don't want your authority, Lena. I want the truth."

Lena was quiet for a moment. Then she said, "Claudette? Are you still there?"

"Yes. I'm sitting in the garden."

"What do you think of it?"

"It's beautiful."

"Yes, it is. And you probably have no idea how hard people had to fight for that space, for the right to bring that beauty into this world. That's my conscience you are looking at. My one good deed."

"Why would you say that? All we do is good deeds. It's one of the perks of the job."

"No. We perform goodness for the public. So long as it doesn't offend, so long as it doesn't require us to stand up for goodness itself. I don't think I really understood the difference between the two things until the purge. You weren't around for that, but I remember. There used to be a space for the garden in the division but over time it just got whittled away. And I went along with that because I wanted to keep my job. But I couldn't be the one responsible for paving it over. So you can judge me if you want, but that garden, in some ways, was my last stand."

Claudette didn't know what to say. She turned again, looked back at the man sitting across from her. There was a whistle tied to a piece of yarn hanging around his neck.

"Perhaps it would be more constructive for you to not worry about that, and just focus on why you're there. I mean why you're really there," Lena said. "Johnson still wants my job and maybe this means he'll get it now. But if he does, there won't be anything I can do for you. So you do what you think is necessary, whatever you need to. I promise, I will stand by you. What's more, I won't forget."

Claudette closed her cell phone.

So there it was. Did it make a difference to Claudette to have her suspicions confirmed, to know her instincts were correct and that the funding to the Center had not been an error but intentional? In some ways it did because at least it meant the situation was not the result of incompetence. If Claudette wasn't able to fix this problem before knowledge of it spread more widely within the company, Lena would be fired. But it wouldn't be because she couldn't handle the responsibilities of her job.

It would be because she'd made a choice.

She looked around her, at the garden. After a while she found herself doing what Lena had advised: she remembered why she was there. She'd agreed to come out of loyalty to her division, but also in exchange for a favor of her own. Claudette had asked for a three-month paid leave to begin exactly six months from the day she requested it. She hadn't gone into detail about why she needed this time, although she and Lena were both women, so she imagined the reason was obvious enough.

She was thirty-seven years old.

"We're handling it, you know."

The man with the orange was speaking to her. He sat pitched forward, Tupperware container balanced on his lap, knees pinched together, smiling.

"Excuse me?"

"The vandalism. That's why you're here, right? From Byrdie's Burgers?" He shook his head. "I bet Millicent sure was surprised to see you walk through the door. She didn't say anything stupid, did she?"

"Stupid? No. Not really."

"Good." The man nodded. "Just checking. She does that sometimes. But you got to understand, we didn't think they had any Black people working there."

Claudette cocked her head in mock surprise. "At Byrdie's Burgers? Really? I thought all Black people worked at Byrdie's Burgers. I thought that was the stereotype."

"You're talking about counter service. Taking your order, flipping your burger, salting your fries. I'm talking about the back rooms, with the people who decide what's actually on the menu these days. Not a lot of us back there I bet. Tell the truth. I bet you're the only one."

"No, sir, I'm not the only one. But you're right. There's not a lot of us, it's true."

The man nodded. "I guess it's up to you then."

"I guess it is."

She watched the man eat his orange.

"Kind of funny, don't you think?" the man said. "I mean we've been here for years, doing what we do, trying to warn people about what's really going on, and nobody paid attention. Haven't had an official visit from corporate in over a decade. And now here you are, on account of some spray-paint scribbles put up by a frustrated child."

"The vandalism? You think a child's been doing it?"

"Well, of course," the man said. "I mean come on. Running around town, crying out for a name? That's a gesture of the young. Besides, can you actually see me running around in the middle of the night, jumping over fences and breaking windows like that? At my age? With my rheumatism?"

Claudette laughed. "I don't think anybody said it was someone at the Center who was actually doing it. My understanding is that Mr. Stone was implying that the work of the Center inspired it."

"Oh, he just doesn't like the fact that we exist is all. But that's not his decision, is it? Mr. Stone doesn't run things. He doesn't even run himself. You gonna shut him up for us?"

"I am. I have a meeting with his manager at the station this afternoon."

"Good." The man nodded and took another bite of his orange. "I mean, it's a start."

Claudette watched the man smile. There was a warmth and calmness that seemed to radiate from his being, which she couldn't help but respond to.

She squinted. "You're Rev Ralston, aren't you?"

"And you are Claudette Adams," Rev said. "Of Byrdie Bird's Family of Friends."

"I thought I recognized you. My parents were huge fans. The Langston Trio was pretty much the soundtrack of my childhood."

"That's nice."

She watched him stand up, pick up a canvas bag lying at his feet, and carry it across the gravel path. He took a seat next to her on the bench and set the bag back down on the ground.

"Now when you go back there, Claudette Adams, just be sure corporate knows the situation is under control. We're handling it. See? So there's no point in getting involved now."

Claudette smiled. Despite his strange words and odd appearance, she found him not just charming, but disarming somehow.

That was how she felt: disarmed.

"Tell corporate to just sit back and keep doing what they've been doing—which isn't much, when you come right down to it," Rev said. "But the vandalism is not what's important. It's just a distraction, an isolated incident, and it will stop soon enough on its own. See? Clearly the boy responsible for it has already accomplished what he set out to do."

"Well, that's good news," Claudette said. "I take it you're in contact with him?"

"Not personally, no." He reached into a satchel at his feet and pulled out another large Tupperware container.

"But you know who it is?"

"What I know is that, whoever it is, they've got the mind of a tactician. And sometimes you have to judge the intention of a tactician by way of the result."

"Is that right?"

"Well, look. He found a way to take a complicated idea and translate it into a simple phrase people can understand. He heard the message the world was giving him, but instead of getting too bogged down by the details of it, answered back with a message of his own. *We will not be erased. We will not be subsumed.* That's what that signage is really saying. And that's powerful. Provoked a reaction. We're getting some real reverberations because of it."

"I see what you mean," Claudette said. "Unfortunately, the only reverberation I'm seeing is a lot of negative attention for the Center."

"Not true." Rev smiled. He nudged her arm with his shoulder. "Brought you here, didn't it, Claudette Adams? Might turn out there's a reason for that."

Then he opened the container on his lap.

"Geezus!" Claudette flinched. As soon as he unsealed the lid it unleashed a scent so powerful it brought tears to her eyes, a smell she immediately recognized as the one she had encountered when she first entered the building. "What is that?" Claudette wheeled her body away from him and winced.

"Lunch," Rev said. "Powerful, isn't it? Little something I came up with, made from ingredients all grown right here in the garden. You want some?"

Claudette shook her head, covering her mouth and nose with one hand while frantically fanning the air with the other.

"Please get that away from me."

He shrugged and put the lid back on the container.

"Thank you," Claudette said, still fanning the air. "I'm sorry, I don't mean to be rude. It's just I haven't been feeling well lately. Been a little sensitive to smells."

"That's all right, Claudette Adams," Rev said. "Nothing wrong with being sensitive. Just means you're human."

He put the Tupperware back in his satchel, then looked at her and smiled. "Which means you've come to the right place." He reached for her hand. "The garden is a sanctuary for all human beings. You are safe here."

"That's nice," Claudette said. She wiped the tears from her eyes. "Thank you for that."

He stood up.

"Everything comes from the garden, Claudette Adams. The garden is your answer and way forward. The garden contains all you'll need."

"I'll remember that." Claudette nodded. "I hope so. . . ."

She watched him walk back inside.

She sat there for a few minutes with her eyes closed and hand covering her mouth and nose, taking a series of deep breaths and waiting for the smell to subside. When it seemed enough time had passed she removed her hand and, very tentatively, began breathing through her nose again.

When she did, a strange thing happened. She could still smell the garlic, but instead of her initial agitation, its lingering presence made her feel strangely calm. It occurred to her that perhaps what had really been bothering her since she entered the Center was not so much the smell itself as the inability to discern its source.

When she was ready, she picked up her briefcase and walked back inside. She found Millicent in the front office and told her good-bye. Then she walked back out to the street.

A boxy tan Buick she'd rented at the airport that morning was parked out front. She got inside, put the briefcase in the back seat, turned a key in the ignition, and started driving.

For the next ten minutes she wound past streets she thought she remembered from an earlier time, streets that felt familiar in their very unfamiliarity, streets she still recalled just well enough to sense how much they'd changed. Before her parents moved to the state capital when she was nine, the Moore Center for Creative Unity had been a part of her childhood, the odd heart of the community she'd only ever half understood and that she mostly recalled as something that was simply there. It had occupied the periphery of her daily life, a strangely pungent evocation of unconditional love that she'd never bothered to pay much attention to. The fact that it could now be considered a threat was, in and of itself, a reflection of how much things had changed. It was just too dangerous these days for a company like Byrdie's Burgers to be seen as endorsing any views that might be considered political and partisan, whereas once, when the original contribution had been made, it had seemed dangerous not to.

The car rolled up an overpass and sped across the interstate that bifurcated the town into north and south sides. Claudette wasn't sure what to make of what Lena had done, whether the secret contributions to the Center represented a covert act of generosity or an overt act of cowardice. Had Lena really thought she was standing up for goodness? Or was she just passing the buck, accepting the inevitable but refusing to take responsibility for it, thereby creating a situation where Claudette had to be brought in to try to clean up her mess?

She wound down an overpass and the car decelerated as she approached a stoplight.

Lena, Claudette knew, must have realized her behavior threatened to put the entire division and the work they did at risk. Because of course the division had started out as a cynical gesture, thought up by a clever marketer to generate free, positive press coverage— possibly the same clever marketer who had somehow instinctively understood that a giant cartoon pigeon was the most effective means of selling hamburgers to children. But it was inaccurate to say that no good came out of it. Over the years the division had helped thousands of families in need. It was just that there were limits to what they could do, a line that had to be walked in order to maintain the ability to do that good, and anyone who couldn't accept that had no business working there. The reputation of the brand was sacrosanct, and if the division ever proved a contradiction to that fact they would be shut down.

She drove through the north side, then wheeled around a corner until she saw the station's call letters on the side of a small concrete building. *Sometimes you couldn't do everything you might have wanted to,* Claudette thought as she pulled up to the curb in front of the station. Sometimes you had to choose whether it was better to do something that represented a compromise or step aside and do nothing at all.

She got out of the car and entered the lobby of the station, where a woman sat behind a large white front desk.

"May I help you?"

"Claudette Adams. I have an appointment with the station manager, Mr. Shannon, at noon."

"He's aware. He'll be with you in a moment."

Claudette looked around the lobby. The walls were lined with black-and-white photographs, all pictures of the same man shaking hands with various pop stars and celebrities, taken when they performed concerts in town. She could tell by the way the man got progressively older in them that they had been arranged in chronological order. Taken together they told a story, if anyone was interested in hearing it.

Claudette already knew parts of it. KQFM began broadcasting back in the 1950s as a beautiful music station. They switched to Urban Contemporary in the early seventies, and for the next twenty years they'd been top-rated in their market. All that abruptly changed in 1992, when WFLA, the local country station, was bought by new owners, who brought in a programming director from out of town. He changed WFLA's moniker from "Cool Breeze of Country" to "the Beast," and immediately switched their format to Urban Contemporary, putting them in direct competition with KQFM. Initially, this didn't seem to make sense because everyone already listened to KQFM, and since both stations were offering the same product, they had no reason to change their dials—but then he gave them one. From the moment "the Beast" hit the airwaves they set out to prove that the success of the station wasn't about the songs they showcased; it was about a battle for hearts and minds. They went on the attack, inaugurated a relentless campaign of abuse and ridicule. They mocked KQFM's DJs, came up with denigrating nicknames for both them and their wives. They prank-called the station, broadcast crude rumors about anyone affiliated with it, even offered prizes for anyone photographed defacing KQFM's call sign while wearing a "the Beast" T-shirt. It was appalling, unprecedented behavior, but it worked. Increasingly the public began to tune in, not to hear the music so much as because they didn't want to miss whatever appalling thing WFLA might do next. The music, it seemed, was beside the point and less than three months after the assault began, WFLA was number one.

It was a brutal and, in some circles, legendary takedown from which KQFM never recovered. They limped along for another few months and then switched to Golden Oldies. In 1994 they were bought out by Translucent Media. Then, in 1996, when the Telecommunications Act made it possible for one company to own multiple stations in a single market, the Beast was acquired by Translucent Media too. The two stations were no longer competitors but different outlets of the same company. WFLA remained the Top 40s station while KQFM broadcast a combination of classic rock and talk radio that made up a full schedule of syndicated programming, save for a single, daily two-hour block of late-night local news, hosted by Edward P. Stone.

A phone rang on the woman's desk. She picked it up, listened for a minute, then set it back down.

"He says for you to just go on in."

Claudette walked through the door behind the front desk and

made her way to Mr. Shannon's office. She found him sitting by him-self, eating a sandwich that smelled very strongly of spoiled bologna and processed cheese.

"Ms. Adams—is that right?" He gestured for her to take a seat across from him. Claudette struggled to breathe through her mouth as she made her way inside the office. "What can I do for you?"

"I'm here about Mr. Stone's broadcast from March 8."

"That's what I thought." Mr. Shannon nodded and took another bite of his sandwich. "Look, I'm already aware of your concerns and as much as I'd like to sit here all day and go over them with you, I do have a station to run. So I'll be blunt. Mr. Stone is not going to recant or apologize for anything he said during his broadcast. The man was expressing his opinions, and he's entitled to those. It's called the First Amendment."

He picked up his sandwich and took another bite.

"There's a difference between opinions and slander. But perhaps that's for a court to adjudicate," Claudette said.

Mr. Shannon sighed. "There was no slander, Ms. Adams. It was commentary. Now you may not like what Mr. Stone says. I may not like what Mr. Stone says. But the fact is he has every right to say it. What's more, if you listen, you'll note our disclaimer at the beginning of each broadcast, which very clearly states that neither the station nor Translucent Media endorse the views expressed by Mr. Stone. It's entertainment."

"Nevertheless, your station and, by default, Translucent Media provide the platform for him to express his views. Which means you are attributing value to it. Some might interpret that as a tacit en-dorsement."

"No. Look, I'm not sure you understand how it works. It's not me that attributes value. It's the audience. Stone's show is very popular and there is a reason for that. The man does not censor himself and people respect that. I understand he can sometimes be a bit rough but that's because he says exactly what's on his mind. He says things people think but feel like they've lost the right to say. He's outlandish, but that's why everybody loves him."

"Not everybody," Claudette said. "Clearly."

"Well, you know what? If that's how you feel? You don't have to listen. That's one of the great things about being in America, don't you think? Freedom of assembly, freedom of choice. If you don't like what Mr. Stone has to say, just change the dial. There are a lot of stations out there for you to listen to. R and B stations, hip-hop stations . . . Feel free to listen to whichever one you choose."

"Right now I'm listening to your station, Mr. Shannon," Claudette said. "The fact is you don't make money from your audience. You make it from your advertisers. Are you not concerned with how your tacit endorsement of Mr. Stone's libelous comments reflect upon the credibility of your brand?"

"My brand?" He laughed. "Oh, come on. I've tried to be nice about this, because I feel for you people, I really do. But there's only so much I can take. Quite frankly I'd suggest you spend less time worrying about my brand, about what Stone has to say, and more time focusing on not giving him a reason to say it."

"Excuse me?"

"It's not a secret you know. What a mess it is over there on the south side. The crime, the drugs, the trash. The gangbangers hanging out on every corner, shooting each other left and right. You think no one has noticed? Has a right to have an opinion about it? Stone didn't create your problems. He's not responsible for them, and neither am I. If you really want to help your people, then maybe it's time to start taking some responsibility instead of blaming everyone else."

Claudette cocked her head and smiled. "Mr. Shannon? I think there's been a miscommunication. Are you aware of who you are speaking to right now? Because you seem to be under the impression that I'm a representative of the Moore Center for Creative Unity."

"Aren't you?"

She reached into the pocket of her blazer and handed him her card. "I represent Byrdie's Burgers Foods."

He looked confused. He stared at the card, checked his calendar, and then looked back at her.

"Oh."

And there it was. A look she'd gotten extremely accustomed to since she'd started working for Byrdie Bird's Family of Friends. The flash of recognition, the sudden realization that someone had lost track of what they were doing, misinterpreted the situation, and gotten something very wrong. She took a breath and then spoke.

"Let me assure you, Mr. Shannon, that Byrdie's Burgers is not interested in your views on affirmative action, social unrest, or urban blight. I'm here to find out why you have chosen to allow one of your hosts to involve a multimillion-dollar food conglomerate and beloved global icon of American culture and values in what seems a rather petty and decidedly local dispute. You also seem a bit confused about the distinction between the expression of a personal opinion and the broadcasting of slander. Fortunately, Byrdie's Burgers has an entire team of lawyers on retainer whose sole function is clarifying that distinction in court.

"Now, it occurs to me, Mr. Shannon, that perhaps because the show is only broadcast regionally, you may have thought we would not notice Mr. Stone's comments. But we did notice. We notice everything, with the same meticulous attention to detail that has made us a market leader. It's why we're number one, Mr. Shannon. And we intend to stay that way. Any effort to impugn the reputation of either the Byrdie's Burgers brand or the Byrdie Bird logo should be considered an invitation for immediate legal action, which we are prepared to ensure continues for as long as it might for us to receive a judgment we deem adequate and fitting. We will sue not only Translucent Media, but you and Mr. Stone personally. By the time we are finished, you and Mr. Stone will come to embody such an enormous financial liability that it goes without saying that neither of you should ever expect to work in broadcasting again. That statement, by the way, is neither an opinion nor slander. It is simply a fact."

Mr. Shannon stared.

"This is all a mistake," he said. "I mean it—the whole thing was just a big misunderstanding. I'm sorry I didn't recognize you when you walked through the door. It's just when you mentioned March 8 I got confused because . . ."

"Because what?"

"Because those Moore people have been all over me about that, ever since the broadcast aired." He blinked. "They're really the ones he was complaining about. Stone mentioned Byrdie's Burgers three times, it's true. But that was just a messaging issue. Stone has nothing against Byrdie's Burgers and neither do I. We love Byrdie's Burgers, same as everyone else. He mentioned it, but he didn't mean it as a criticism. It just came out wrong. One of the callers picked up on it, so it went on for a little longer than it should have. But that wasn't the point he was trying to make."

"What point was he trying to make?"

Mr. Shannon shook his head. "We were being considered for syndication. I told him when he reports on this local stuff, he should look for ways to signal broader relevance. We were trying to make it easier for Translucent to conceptualize our national appeal."

"Excuse me?" Claudette squinted. "Are you saying that broadcast was a demo reel?"

"It was a fuck up, okay? But we were desperate. I mean look around you. Syndication has wrecked this station, but now it's the only way out. That's the reality and it's not even about a choice. It's a matter of survival. But rest assured we already got pretty much the same talk from Translucent that you're giving me now. Lesson learned. It's how you know I'm telling the truth when I say to you it won't happen again."

Claudette nodded. "Where did he get that information from, by the way? About Byrdie Bird's sponsorship?"

"Who the fuck knows? It was an idiotic thing to bring up, although, honestly, if you think about it, you guys should just take it as a compliment."

"Why is that?"

"In terms of signaling appeal. I asked him to find ways to make these stories seem universal and there's only a few brands out there that can really message that. Coca-Cola, Disney, Byrdie's Burgers. You guys are pretty much it. You're not just an American product anymore. You're an actual American ideal."

Claudette walked back out to her car.

That, she thought, was the power of integration. What it meant to be a part of the Byrdie's Burgers family. It meant you never walked alone, that when you spoke you had the power of an entire corporation to amplify your words. Also, in her case, it often meant that people did not seem to recognize that fact until she explained it to them.

She climbed inside the driver's seat. It had happened before. Often, she just let people talk—it was perversely fascinating to watch people dig their own graves. The way they sometimes just kept digging long after it should have been clear who she was, what she represented, why she was there. Mr. Shannon assumed she was from the Moore Center because she was Black. And Black, despite the decades of Black people putting the time in, smiling behind counters and asking others what they could get for them today, was not, in truth, what Byrdie's Burgers looked like.

She put the key in the ignition and started the car. It had happened before; it happened a lot. Sometimes she told herself that these encounters ultimately provided her with a great deal of useful information. Because people—both Black and white—had a tendency to reveal things about themselves to her that they would have never shown her coworkers in the division. Sometimes she told herself that, given the specific nature of her work, this behavior she tended to provoke in others was an asset, part of why she was so good at her job. Because it provided her with what she'd decided was valuable insight into how the initiatives they sponsored actually treated the people who walked through their doors.

Other times it just made her feel nauseous.

Claudette pushed open the door as she found herself struck by a sudden strong wave of sickness, and then vomited onto the street. She sat like that for a full five minutes, pitched forward as she convulsed violently. When at last the feeling subsided she sat back up, leaned against the headrest, and shut her eyes.

This too would pass, she told herself. The nausea, the sensitivity to smells . . . It was all perfectly normal, and eventually would stop. She tried to focus on her breathing, tried to think calming thoughts, and found her mind drifting back to her time in the garden, listening to Rev's voice telling her that she was safe, that it was all right to be human and to simply feel.

She was just about to pull away from the curb when she looked up and realized there were people on the sidewalk, staring at her. She realized she had just vomited on the street, but none of them spoke to her or asked her if she was okay. They were eyeing her, not out of concern or out of sympathy for a woman who was clearly not well and doing her best to keep going.

Instead, they were eyeing her with suspicion.

She looked away from them and started driving the car, headed back towards the south side.

She drove until she reached the Byrdie's Burgers franchise just at the northern edge of the interstate. This was the final piece of the puzzle, the actual star of this shit show she'd found herself compelled to make an appearance in. The franchises were, after all, what it was all about. She pulled into the parking lot and wheeled the Buick past the long line of cars that snaked around the side of the restaurant to the drive-thru window. When she walked inside she felt immediately comforted by a blast of air conditioning and an interior composed of the familiar and strangely soothing mix of orange and yellow. It was crowded, and she was struck by the mix of customers filling out the space around her. There was a place for everyone at Byrdie's Burgers. Excited children eating hamburgers as they sat with their grandparents, fast-talking middle school girls in cheerleader uniforms sipping chocolate milkshakes, teens in corner booths laughing as they lobbed french fries at each other. Standing at the counter, a man in work boots, paint-splattered pants, and a hard hat still tucked under his arm was placing his order while behind him, a man in a business suit was talking on a cell phone and calmly waiting for his turn. For all the complaints about both their products and their business practices, the restaurants themselves really were democratic, corporate-sponsored spaces, more so than any other institution she could think of at the time. This franchise in particular, being located in what was considered a border zone, had a very diverse customer base as, despite technically being on the north side, it got a lot of south side traffic from people headed to and from their places of work. What's more, it was immaculate and clearly well-maintained, despite the fact that it smelled overwhelmingly like pickles and hot ketchup.

She made her way to the counter and stood before an officious-looking Black teenager.

"Welcome to Byrdie's Burgers. What can I get for you today?"

Claudette told him her name and that she had an appointment with the franchise's owner/operator. He jogged around back and then returned a few minutes later with a tall, thin man in his sixties trailing behind him. The man introduced himself as Todd Radcliffe. Todd led her past the counter, down a short hallway, and into his small office behind the kitchen.

"I appreciate you taking the time to meet with me before you make any decisions about how to handle the fallout from the vandalism," Todd said.

"Not at all. After all, you're the real reason I'm here. One of our main concerns, even within the charitable division, is to always show support for our franchises."

Todd nodded. "If that's true, if the stability of the franchise is really what you care about, then respectfully, I'm going to ask you to stand down."

The situation, Todd told her, was already under control. He'd had the restaurant repainted and coated with an anti-graffiti prepolymer. He was in the process of installing more security cameras, both inside the restaurant and out. There was no need for any further action to be taken by corporate. And certainly, under no circumstances, should they discontinue funding to the Center.

"You all haven't been paying much attention to what's been going on in that place, have you?"

"Apparently not as much as we should have."

"Well, whatever you might be thinking of doing, I'm asking you not to do it now. If you were to cut ties with the Center now or do anything that might lead to it shutting down because of something Edward Stone said on the radio, it could very well provoke a boycott."

"You think that's a legitimate concern?"

"I think it's a real possibility, yes I do. It definitely could do it. In fact it's probably one of the few things that could. Furthermore, I think it's the whole point."

He told her he knew exactly who was doing the vandalizing: a former employee by the name of Calvin Green. Calvin's uncle had owned the franchise back in the 1980s; he was killed in a car accident when Calvin was twelve years old and thereafter the boy developed what Todd described as an unnatural attachment to the place. The restaurant had switched hands two more times before Todd bought it, at which point Calvin was already working there.

"Now I knew he was kind of weird the first time I talked to him but I let him stay because it seemed like the kind of weird that would work to my advantage. He took everything about the job with the utmost seriousness and it goes without saying he was a hard worker and always on time. What's more, it was clear that he genuinely loved the place. Not just the franchise, but Byrdie's Burgers as a whole. He talked about this place like it was his home, like Byrdie Bird was his family. But everything started to go south the first time I happened to mention I was thinking about retiring. Do you know, I think that crazy boy actually thought he could just slip in and take over somehow? Eventually I had to explain to him that wasn't how it worked. I sat him down and went over the actual financials involved. Things have changed since his uncle ran the place. I explained how market saturation meant more competition, but also made it a lot more expensive to buy in. He didn't have the resources for the down payment and there was no way he would ever qualify for a loan. Really, I was trying to help, encourage him to focus on his education, maybe go to business school and then work on building up a portfolio. But maybe it came out too harsh. I figure he kind of snapped after that, which, in retrospect, I should have seen coming."

Claudette nodded. "So you feel you are being specifically targeted? Because my understanding is that the attacks have been pervasive, that the vandalism has been occurring all over the city, not just here."

"Yes. Because he's smart. Trying to sow chaos and confusion, draw more attention to his actions while, at the same time, obscuring his actual intent. And it worked, didn't it? I mean, you are, in fact, here."

"But why?"

"Because he's trying to devalue the franchise. I figure he thinks it's the only way he can get his hands on something that, in his mind, is already his," Todd said. "I've never known anyone more attached to a brand. He knew everything about the company, was like our in-house Encyclopedia Brown. Did I know Byrdie's Burgers was the largest employer of Black youth in America? Did I know there were over 1,700 Byrdie's Burgers franchises spread out across the country? Did I know Byrdie Bird's Family of Friends began in 1974 with a single initiative in Philadelphia and since that time has grown to 375 locations in 64 countries?"

Claudette looked up.

"That's right. As soon as I heard Stone had mentioned Byrdie Bird's Family of Friends during his broadcast I got suspicious. Why would Stone know who was sponsoring the Moore Center, unless someone told him? But Calvin? He knew more about the company than even I did. Maybe even knew more about it than you."

He shook his head. "The boy is a terrorist. That's all there is to it. And right now, he's holding this franchise hostage, whether you realize it or not. He knows what that Center means to people around here. And he knows that if Byrdie's Burgers were to abandon them now, after all Edward Stone has been saying about the south side, this franchise would bear the brunt of the fallout from that. He's a terrorist and sometimes terrorists are smart. Which means the only way to deal with them is to be smart too."

Claudette shook his hand and thanked him for his insight into the situation. Then she walked back to her car.

As she drove towards the hotel where she was staying that night, she wasn't sure what to make of her conversation with Todd Radcliffe. The idea that the vandalism was, in truth, a manifestation of some elaborate scheme was not something she'd ever considered. Who knew if it was true, if the man was being paranoid or not? She wasn't sure how much it even mattered, as the intentions of the vandal did not account for the risk posed by the Center itself. She wondered if she had, for the first time in her career, stumbled into a situation where the stability of a single franchise would have to be sacrificed for the sake of the many.

Her room at the Hyatt Regency smelled like talcum powder and cleaning products, and she'd barely had time to set her bag on the bed when she heard her cell phone ring again.

She pressed a button.

"You haven't been answering my calls. Why the hell haven't you been answering my calls?"

"Please calm down," she told her husband. "I'm working. That's all."

"And where are you now?"

"I just checked into a hotel."

Claudette sat down on the edge of the bed and took her shoes off. "You know it's funny. I still remember when people didn't have cell phones. They were supposed to be liberating because you could talk whenever you want, but it also seems to mean I'm supposed to be available all hours of the day, no matter what else I'm doing, what else is going on. Sometimes it feels like I'm just carrying around a portable surveillance system."

"You were supposed to come back this afternoon."

"Yes, well, it turns out the situation here is a bit complicated. It's going to take at least another day to sort out."

"What about your doctor's appointment? You do realize you missed another doctor's appointment."

"Couldn't be avoided." She lay back on the bed. "But don't worry, I'll make another appointment for next week."

"You can't keep missing appointments, Claudette," her husband said. "It's not just you I'm worried about. You have to think about someone else too now."

Claudette stared up at the ceiling.

"Claudette? You're geriatric."

"Yes. I'm aware. But thank you for bringing it up again."

"It's not an opinion or a judgment. It's a medical fact. All pregnancies past the age of thirty-five are geriatric. It means you have to take it easy whether you want to or not. You've got to stop working so much, find ways to relax."

"That is why I'm working so much now, remember? So I can take a break."

"Honestly? I don't see how what you're doing now is any different from what you've always done. That's who you are. You work. Sometimes I wonder if you are really prepared for how much that is going to have to change. Otherwise, I just don't understand what we're doing."

Claudette was quiet.

"Yes. I've realized that about you," she said. "There are a lot of things you don't seem to understand. And yet they are still real."

"Is this even something you want, Claudette? Because if you can't stop working to take care of yourself, how do you really expect to be able to take care of someone else?"

Claudette pressed a button and put down the phone.

She stared at the ceiling. He hadn't said anything she didn't already know. She did love her job. She was good at it and, if she was honest, knew that if it ever came down to a choice between her husband and her work, she would choose the latter. Did that make her a bad person? A bad wife? A bad woman? Did it mean she was destined to be a bad mother too?

What if she did bring a child into this world only to find out she lacked the capacity to actually love it? What if she lacked the patience and fortitude that being a good mother seemed to require? And if she didn't know then what was she doing?

There was, in some ways, a clear contradiction in the fact that she was working so hard just to be able to take time away from work. Was this really what she even wanted? Or just something she'd always thought she was supposed to want?

Sometimes she wasn't certain. Sometimes all she could think about was what it would mean for her career. Was that wrong to think about those things? To even acknowledge she was aware of them?

A window was closing; she was aware of that too—but did that mean she had to jump out of it now? How could she know if the timing was right? How could she know if she was making the right choice or even what that choice would actually mean?

She couldn't.

She sat up on the bed. She reminded herself that, in some ways, it was already a moot point. Somehow a combination of anxiety, insecurity, and indecision had carried her far enough along that, legally, there was no turning back now. It wasn't a question of deciding anymore; it was decided. Whatever she was doing, was already done.

She stood up and carried her briefcase to the small desk by the window. She pulled out her IBM ThinkPad. Instead of worrying about the future, she decided to focus on what she was good at, the one thing she was fully confident she knew how to do.

She did her job.

• • •

THE FOLLOWING AFTERNOON, CLAUDETTE DROVE back to the Center and met with Millicent in the main office.

"Good news." Claudette smiled. "I am happy to report that we at Byrdie's Burgers would like to reaffirm our commitment to the Center. In fact, we'd like to increase our financial support, provide you with additional resources."

"Really? That's wonderful!"

"Yes, this visit has confirmed what a vital part of your community your organization is. A much beloved institution, and we would like to see it remain a part of this community. Unfortunately, as the incident with Mr. Stone has shown, the type of work you do seems particularly vulnerable to attack and misrepresentation. Which means the problem is not with you, per se, but rather one of messaging. I'd like to help with that too."

"What does that mean?"

Claudette nodded to a banner that read "More Justice for Moore People." "When you look at that, Millicent, what do you see?"

"I see the truth. What we stand for, why we're here."

"Yes," Claudette said. "I see that too. But you know what else I see? The past. A time when we faced real, concrete barriers. A time, not so long ago, where there were signs not just in this city but all over the country that said 'No Blacks Allowed.' A time when there were many people in power in this country who claimed that Black people weren't just inferior but dangerous. That somehow, their sense of their own superiority gave them the right to brutalize us. When Leon Moore hung up that banner, he was giving his response. He was telling the world that, despite the lies they'd been told, we were human beings. We were a people of strength and beauty, a people of value, who would fight for the right to express it. He was a brave man who was willing to stand up for justice and goodness, and as a result of his efforts and the efforts of thousands of men and women like him, those signs came down. Which means you and I are now operating in a new reality, Millicent."

She pointed back to the banner. "That message make sense within a framework that doesn't actually exist anymore. It belongs to another world."

Millicent frowned. "Maybe that's true for you, but from where I'm standing it doesn't seem like things have changed all that much. Yes, they took down the signs. But sometimes it feels like that's all they did."

"Yes, that's exactly my point, Millicent. They took the signs down and then they didn't replace them. The same barriers still exist, but they've gone underground so you can only truly see them in terms of their varied effects. This lack of clear messaging has caused a certain amount of confusion and panic, but also, for our purposes, it means the terms of engagement have changed. In order to be effective, we've got to change too."

"What exactly are you talking about?"

"I'm talking about the garden," Claudette said. "Now, I was up all night thinking about this and I think the garden is the answer, our way forward. From now on, when people ask you what you stand for, don't point to a banner. Instead direct them to the garden outside."

"But why?"

"You ever heard of a man named Phil Sokolof? He's a wealthy industrialist who, about ten years ago, had a heart attack after eating too many Byrdie's Burgers. Somehow he decided the entire fast-food industry was responsible for his own poor choices and poor health. He went on a crusade against cholesterol, obesity, diabetes—he's already spent close to a million dollars of his own money paying for ads about all the things the industry is doing wrong. Weirdly, it's had an impact. Now everyone is falling over themselves to pitch some sort of nutritional value for their products—which there isn't, by the way. You really shouldn't eat that stuff. But the point is, for our purposes, Byrdie Bird becoming a sponsor for the community garden just makes sense. Or I can make it make sense. It's going to be a way to redirect conversation, to demonstrate a positive impact both on nutrition and the environment, and deflect from the damage caused by our actual product itself."

"You think that will do something?"

"Absolutely," Claudette said. "I spent most of this morning going back and forth with marketing on email. I wanted to gauge their reaction, and it turns out the idea of expanding the Family's mandate to include community gardens in inner cities was something everyone is enthusiastic about. It's the future and could be a model for not only this center but further investment in other communities."

"But it's not really accurate," Millicent said. "I mean, we're not just about the garden, that's not all we do. We're about preserving the community. The garden exists because the community needs it."

"Well, the garden needs the community too. I mean it's true, right? I'm just asking you to turn it around in your mind. Instead of talking about why the garden is necessary for the community, I want you to think about how the community is necessary for the garden and what that actually means." Claudette smiled. "It's perfect. Don't you see? I'm not trying to change what you do. I'm trying to reframe it. I'm trying to make it possible for you to keep doing it by coming up with a strategy for talking about it in a language the public will understand and that Byrdie Bird can actually endorse." She frowned. "Which brings me to another matter. In order for this to happen you are going to have to officially join the Family of Friends."

"Join? But I thought we already were part of the Family."

"No, Millicent. Official membership means changing the name. Instead of the Moore Center, you have to become a franchise of Byrdie Bird's Family of Friends. But before you say anything, just listen to me, because I think I've worked out some ways for you to think of it as less of an erasure and more as a transference."

She took a deep breath.

"First. I'd like to put Byrdie Bird's name out front and then formally dedicate the garden to Leon Moore. And I will allocate funds for a statue of Moore that we would put right in the middle of it. You'll be able to maintain the space as the sanctuary he intended, and it will remain named in his honor in perpetuity. Second. I'm going to get the name of this street changed. I've already had some communication with a few members of your city council, and I think we're very close to negotiating a compromise. They can't rename the entire street, but they can designate the surrounding block as a plaza, which will be named in Leon Moore's honor."

"They agreed to that?"

"They will. Yes. You go along with this plan and his name will still be everywhere. Just not above the door of the Center itself."

"Wow," Millicent said. She shook her head. "This is a lot. I need some time to think about it. Need to talk to the others."

"Understood. But I'm going to have to ask you to talk fast. I'm afraid I'm going to need an answer by the end of the day."

"End of the day? How can you expect me to turn around and agree to something this big that quick? When all of this is coming out of nowhere?"

"It's not coming out of nowhere, Millicent," Claudette said. "It's coming from me. Now, I have spent the past twenty-four hours working on this, and I was able to come up with a solution most people would not have thought possible. Quite frankly, you should consider yourselves fortunate that Lena sent me here and not someone else, that I agreed to take this assignment. No one else in my division would have cared enough or been able to do the same."

"Lena?" Millicent snorted. "Who the heck is Lena? I don't even know who that woman is anymore. The Lena Rev always talks about would have come here herself."

"What do you mean, 'the Lena Rev always talks about'?"

Millicent shook her head and pointed to the group photo hanging on the wall. "That's the Lena Rev knew, the one I thought I was talking to, every time she called."

Claudette squinted at the picture. In the background, wearing the same T-shirt and bell-bottoms as the others on the bridge, was a young chubby white woman with a short brown bob.

"All these years, that's who I thought I was talking to," Millicent said. "But she's not here anymore, is she?"

"No," Claudette said. "I am."

She picked up her briefcase and started walking towards the metal doors.

"I'll give you some time to think."

• • •

AN HOUR LATER SHE WAS sitting in the garden, going over the details of her new strategy when she heard a voice call out to her.

"Millicent told me about your plan."

Rev was standing over her.

"What do you think?"

"I think it's smart. I mean I get it. And more importantly, I think you get it too."

He sat down on the bench beside her.

"Fascinating, isn't it? All that stuff about walls shifting form, barriers going underground. Signs being rendered invisible. How do you think they managed that?"

"I don't know. Just an effect of the times. It's not like everyone wanted to take the signs down. Certainly not the people who put them up. The signs came down because they had to."

"No, but specifically. How did they do it?"

He leaned close to her ear.

"I'm talking about the cloaking device. I mean supposedly we don't have that kind of technology yet. Where do you think they acquired the ability to render themselves invisible? Unless it's alien technology."

He smiled and she smiled back, even though she didn't get the joke.

After a while she stopped smiling.

"What do you mean, 'alien'?"

"You're a smart woman, Claudette. And I believe you were sent here for a reason. I believe you have the capacity to handle the truth, to comprehend that really, it's the only explanation that makes sense." He shook his head. "You've never actually seen one, have you?"

"No," Claudette said. "Have you seen one?"

"Yes. But only twice. Managed to catch it unawares. First time was about sixteen years ago. I had a break from touring and was hanging out with Leon; Shay was there too. We were walking across a bridge and found ourselves confronted by a couple of crackers. They were threatening to do something bad, I don't even remember what, we used to get so many threats back then; it was hard to keep track. But then, while they were shouting at us, I happened to look up and realized there was something behind them. Something lurking in the shadows. It was big and hairy and green, with eyes and a mouth but no ears. And the weird thing was, its lips were moving soundlessly right along with the men who were shouting at us, like somehow it was dictating their words and the things it was saying were coming out of their mouths. Almost like they were puppets.

"Scared the heck out of me but Moore must have seen it too. Had the sense to pick up a rock and throw it at it. Realizing that its manipulations had been detected, it scattered off into the night, just like that, its puppet men chasing right after it. I have had to deal with knowing it was there ever since. And of course, that changed everything."

Claudette stared. "What?"

Rev smiled. "I'm telling you the truth, Claudette. Because I think you can handle it. There's an interstellar conflict going on right now, and this here is the front lines. This garden is key, Claudette, to the fate of humanity."

"Okay." Claudette nodded. "Is Millicent aware of all of this?"

"Of course she is. She was there too."

"Where?"

"Not the first time I saw it, but the last time. Back on that bridge. I'd been trying everything I could think of to make it reveal itself again, and finally something worked. And Millie just happened to be out on that bridge that night too; don't ask me what she was doing. But that's how we met her." He smiled. "You should have seen her back then, boy. That woman was a total mess, but I tell you what, she's been cold sober ever since that night. That's what happened to all of us. Her, me, Shay, Leon . . . Every one of us who saw it. None of us have been the same since. Because we know what the stakes are."

He reached into his pocket. "And now that you know, you're gonna need something to protect yourself."

He pulled out a whistle.

"Now these beings, they might keep to the shadows. But believe you me, they are always there. And truth is they don't respond well to knowing they've been detected. For your protection, I would suggest you keep this with you at all times."

He placed the whistle in her palm, then patted her on the shoulder, stood up, and walked back inside.

Claudette watched him go, stunned. As she tried to make sense of Rev's words, she found herself thinking about some of the things she had seen at the Center the day before: the child's drawing of the monster, the women in the robes, the strange hand signals at the door. It occurred to her that these details had presented her with a possibility she hadn't bothered to consider at the time but perhaps should have.

What if it was a cult?

She looked around the garden. She had submitted her proposal without actually having any idea what was going on at the Center. It was entirely possible it was a cult. She had no way of knowing for certain but one thing was clear: if it was true, then in all likelihood she was about to be fired.

She leaned forward and vomited.

"You all right?" Shay was standing over her.

"No. I'm not," Claudette said. "I'm going to just come out and ask you a question and I'd like you to tell me the truth. Is this a cult?"

"Is what a cult?"

"This. The garden. Rev, Millicent. All of it."

"You've been talking to Rev, haven't you?" Shay rolled her eyes and sighed. "He was talking about the alien, wasn't he? I have asked him to not do that."

"I just put my reputation on the line for this Center. I came up with a way to account for all of it. But aliens? No. Not even I can fix that."

"You shouldn't listen to Rev. What he says is not important. Nobody believes him anyhow."

"Is it a cult or not?"

"I don't know what you mean by cult. What is a cult?"

"I think a group of people who believe they are under assault by aliens would certainly qualify. I think that sounds like a cult to me."

"Is that right? Because I thought a cult was a group of people who had lost the ability to think for themselves. Who'd been manipulated into serving the interests of a charismatic leader as opposed to their own. Is that conformity? Or a successful franchise?"

"What?"

"How many people have to belong to the cult for it to become a religion? How many people have to hold a fringe view for it to become an orthodoxy? What makes a successful franchise anyway?"

"What are you talking about?"

"I'm asking because you live in a society that has the idea that one Black person is three-fifths of a human being inscribed in its constitution. A society that believed that because certain people were born female, they were too feeble-minded to vote. You live in a world where people believe skin tone gives them special powers, and that those powers somehow justify them to brutalize other people for doing something as simple as trying to plant a seed. How is that any less crazy than anything Rev has to say? Who the heck are you to judge Rev? Are you rational? Do you know your own mind? How much of what you believe makes sense? How much of what you tell yourself you want is something you actually do want? Or is it just something someone told you that you wanted? Do you even know?"

"Stop! Please!" Claudette felt nauseous again. She clutched her stomach and shook her head. "I'm not trying to insult you. I just want the truth. I need to know what is going on here."

"The answer is no, Ms. Adams. I am not in any cult," Shay said. "Nobody controls my mind but me."

Claudette nodded. "Okay. That's all I wanted to hear. Because he told me you saw it too."

"Yeah, well . . . I know the night he's talking about. And yes, I saw something. The thing is, Rev and me, we have never really agreed on what it was."

"So long as you know it was not an alien."

"Oh, it was an alien all right. It's just I don't think it was an accident that we saw it. See? That first time, with Leon? That was a very particular moment in the movement. We had acquired a certain amount of momentum in terms of what we were trying to accomplish and somehow the timing of this 'discovery' proved a very effective means of disrupting that. It occurred to me, even while I was standing there looking at it, that maybe that was the point. That maybe it had chosen that moment to reveal itself in order to throw us off our game." She shook her head.

"It was suspicious, is what I'm trying to say," Shay said. "And it turned out I was right. Because look what happened. Moore wandered off, started doing his own thing, talking all that wild shit, and wound up getting himself locked up. Rev got obsessed with defense. Meanwhile, what has really changed? There is still so much work to do, still people that need help right here and right now. It was a distraction, just like it was meant to be."

She frowned. "Thing is, I should probably warn you. Some of what he says is true. They do watch us. They watch us all the time. It's just I choose to ignore them and I would suggest you do the same. Still . . ."

She reached into her bag, pulled out another one of Rev's hand-crafted whistles, and handed it to Claudette.

"I don't know if you'll ever need it. Can't say for sure if it even works. But you should probably keep one in your pocket. Just in case."

The Night Nurses

(2004)

It's all better now, and I know I am fortunate. But of course they wouldn't just let us leave. Instead they made us sit there, in a dank little hospital room with hideous green walls and fluorescent lights hovering beneath the low ceiling like depression. Until the doctor came in to do his rounds, sometime around eleven.

I'd been up since five when those three awful night nurses came to check my daughter's vitals and then berated me for giving her apple juice.

"Don't you realize this is a laxative?" one of them said. A lumpy, middle-aged white woman with a mole sprouting hair hanging off her left cheek. I was so exhausted by then it was an effort just to keep my eyes open. I sat there, struggling to focus, while she shook the empty bottle in my face.

"I thought I was supposed to be pushing fluids," I said. "And she wouldn't drink the Pedialyte."

"Just get her cleaned up so we can change these bed linens," the second nurse said. A pale, prune-faced woman with hair standing on top of her head in stiff gray loops, as if she'd removed her curlers before leaving for work and then forgotten to comb it out. Next to her was the third, a girl in her twenties with a greasy blonde ponytail pulled back from her acne-scarred face. She didn't say anything, just stood there with her arms folded in front of her chest and gave my daughter a pitying look.

I staggered to my feet, grabbed the baby wipes, and stumbled to Mahalia's bedside. All three of the night nurses stood behind me and waited as I cleaned off her butt and legs.

It was humiliating. I mean, I knew I'd made a mistake. I'd given her apple juice. But was it really that bad? Didn't they realize I'd been up all night? What right did they have to judge me?

My mind reeled back to just a few hours before, when I'd first stumbled through those emergency room doors with Mahalia in my arms, her breathing just a hoarse moan whispered in my ear.

"Help me," I'd cried.

Those same three nurses rushed into the lobby, squinted at my daughter, and promised everything would be okay.

"Let's get her inside," the one with the mole said. They led us down a hall and into the examination room. But when I tried to lower Mahalia onto the table she let out a tremendous wail, as if terrified I was going to leave her there.

"Oh, no, baby, we just want to look," the second nurse said. But Mahalia kept her body braced against mine, rigid with fear of the unknown.

"It's not so bad if she's still making tears," the one with the pony-tail confided. She backed away from us, nodding and smiling, all three of them talking in loud animated voices that blended in and out with my daughter's screams.

Then someone remembered the Barney video. They all started talking about the Barney video, and I turned around and saw the prune-faced woman wheel an ancient VCR into the room on a cart. The cabinet above the sink was opened and one of them found a video with the familiar face of a purple dinosaur on the box.

"See? It's okay."

Mahalia looked at the TV screen. After a while the pressure of her grip slackened and I leaned forward and eased her onto the table. The night nurses lifted her shirt and took turns placing their hands on her stomach.

One of them wheeled in the IV cart. Another one said, "Keep her still." A third reached for my daughter's hand and fingered the skin along her forearm. I put my arms around Mahalia's shoulders and held her to my chest while she twisted her head back and forth in a nervous smear of mucus and tears that seeped through the front of my shirt.

I held my breath and said nothing. But I saw the way their fingers shook when they stuck Mahalia with that long needle not once but three times before they found a "good vein," a difficulty they swore was common with a child suffering from dehydration. I put my trust in these women and felt nothing but relief when they put Mahalia on that IV drip and wheeled her into the recovery room.

Now I was not so sure. *What kind of credentials did these women actually have?* I wondered. What made them feel they had the right to stand around and shake their heads at me? And of course I wondered if they really talked to everyone like that. Because people do stereotype; it's just naive to think they don't. I'd run out of the house in sweatpants and an old T-shirt, stumbled through those emergency room doors in a desperate panic. I could have been anyone and couldn't help but wonder if they would have talked to me like that if I'd come in dressed for work and looking more like myself.

I changed my daughter's Pull-Up and they changed the bed linens and then left the two of us alone again.

I looked at Mahalia.

"See? Everything's fine. Mommy's right here."

Mahalia shut her eyes. I lay down on the couch next to her bed. But I couldn't sleep. I stared at the ceiling and, for a long time, all I could think about was the way those nurses looked at me when they held up that bottle of apple juice.

Just before dawn there was a knock on the door and one of the orderlies wheeled in Mahalia's breakfast tray. I lifted the plastic cover and what do you think I saw? Apple juice. It turned out that all they had to offer patients was apple juice or milk.

When I heard that I was furious. For a moment I thought about pressing the attendant button and asking the nurses to come gather around so I could show it to them. But then I looked at Mahalia and thought, *Don't do that. Don't let Mahalia see you lose your cool.* Because who were they really, when you came right down to it? Just a group of night nurses in a dingy second-rate hospital.

Besides, the moment had passed. If I called them back now they'd probably tell themselves I was just another hysterical Black mother, getting loud and flying off the handle without the least provocation. They'd tell me that I'd misunderstood, that they were only trying to do their jobs, that all they'd wanted was to change the linens. I realized I already knew the things they would say and so I didn't need to actually hear them.

I went to the bathroom and when I flicked on the light, I saw a cockroach crawl up the wall. I stepped on it and left it lying just inside the bathroom door because I wanted to make sure that when they bent down to clean it up, they would know I'd seen it too.

Mahalia was obviously feeling better by then, laughing and singing songs. Still, they wouldn't let us go home until the doctor signed us out. So we sat in that room for a very long time. Just the two of us.

• • •

ALVIN CAME IN AROUND TEN THIRTY, arms outstretched and full of big sloppy kisses that don't really do anyone much good. Mahalia loves him, of course. As soon as she saw him she threw out her arms.

"Daddy! Daddy!"

"How's my big girl?" He bent down and held her to his chest. I watched him rock her back and forth for a full minute, as if he couldn't think of a single thing except how happy he was to see her.

Yet I must have called him seven times the night before, before I gave up and left a message: *You might want to stop by the hospital when you get a chance. . . .*

Finally he looked at me. "My phone was turned off. Sorry."

"Don't apologize," I said.

He braced himself. I'm sure he thought I was going to start with him, but I wasn't: too tired. All I meant was that I didn't want to hear it.

"It's all better now," I said. They'd determined by then that it was just a nasty virus Mahalia had picked up and that the worst of it was no doubt over.

"I know, I talked to the nurses before I came in." He reached behind him and held up a large shopping bag. "I thought you might want these."

Inside the bag were a change of clothes, my makeup kit, and my toothbrush. When I left my message I'd forgotten to ask him to bring them.

"Were you up all night?"

"Just about." I snatched the bag from his hand. I stepped over the cockroach as I walked into the bathroom and shut the door behind me.

"Honey?" I could hear Alvin calling from the other side. "I really am sorry. . . ."

I flicked on the lights. Things were not going well. There were bags under my eyes and little gray hairs had started popping out in stray curls around my face. I'd put on a lot of weight since Mahalia was born and could see it in places that struck me as odd, like the folds of skin around my neck. *Am I just getting old?* I asked myself. *Is that all it is?* Then I remembered the ugly, haggard light I happened to be standing in. I wondered if the lighting in hospitals was so ugly in an effort to remind people why they were there.

"Honey?" Alvin kept calling through the door. "Are you sure you're all right?"

I reached into the bag, took off my sweatpants and changed into the clothes Alvin had brought. I brushed my teeth and opened my makeup kit. Sometime during the night it had occurred to me that I probably needed to call my lawyer, finish that conversation I'd started then stopped a few months before about the separation of assets. But first I was going to make an appointment to get my hair done. Whatever else happened, I needed to maintain the appearance of stability for my daughter's sake, which was to say, for myself. Artifice was everything; I had no illusions about that anymore.

"I took the morning off," Alvin said when I walked back out.

"Good," I said. "You stay here until the doctor comes. I've got to go out for a while. There are some things I need to take care of."

"Why? I mean, can't it wait? I was hoping we could talk."

"About what?" We'd been married for fifteen years. I'd already heard everything Alvin had to say, and it was all very boring.

"Okay," he said and shut his eyes. "You do whatever you need to do. . . ."

I stared at him. We didn't really have secrets anymore. We pretended we did, but that was just to pass the time. The truth was I knew very well where he was the night before and with whom. I knew her name and I knew where she lived. I knew that if it had come right down to it, if those nurses hadn't been able to find a "good vein" or get Mahalia on that IV and I'd really needed Alvin, then she was the one I would have called.

And he knew it too.

"I love you," Alvin said.

I looked at Mahalia.

You grow up, you get older. Love and gratitude come to you in phases and sometimes come to an end. What changed was not the nature of illusions but your relationship to them. At some point you realized that you wanted to survive, that sometimes survival itself was an act of love.

But it was also an act.

"Mommy will be back soon."

On my way out I passed by the nurses' station. The night nurses were gone now and the woman sitting there was someone I hadn't seen before. She straightened up as soon as she saw me heading towards her. I took one look at her and knew what was true: where the night nurses saw fat and flustered, this one saw formidable and firm.

"May I help you?"

"I certainly hope so. There's a filthy cockroach in my daughter's room, carrying who knows what kind of germs. It's absolutely disgusting. Clean it up."

Trash

(2005)

Raymond Brown sits in the easy chair, staring at a large water stain on his living room ceiling. He lowers his gaze, smiles at the young couple seated across from him on the couch, and says, "She'll be out in a minute. Now, please, don't tell her I told you. Act like you don't even notice."

The young couple stare back and nod stiffly. They glance towards the bathroom door, expecting the worst and wondering what that might be.

"It was never really a problem before," Raymond confides. "But now it's like an obsession with her. Ever since she had the baby." He sips his glass of wine and thinks about his wife Mathilda's smiles and frowns. For the past year he's watched her moods rise and fall in irrational surges, as if keyed to some internal tide pattern. When she was still pregnant there was something endearing about it, like she was channeling the voice of the child inside her, preparing him for things to come.

"But she's so thin," says the woman on the couch. "You'd never even know she had a baby."

"Just try telling her that. I mean it: just try."

After the drugs wore off the first thing Mathilda asked him to do was escort her to the bathroom and hold her arm as she eased onto the scale. He knew she just wanted her "old self" back. But did she really think that "baby weight" meant the weight of an actual child?

No, no. Mathilda shook her head sadly as she stared at the numbers ticking on the scale. Of course not. But there was all that other stuff too: afterbirth, placenta, and whatever else, the accumulated weight, which she somehow expected to come rushing out of her in a flood. When she was still pregnant Raymond might have encouraged such delusions, might have thought it best to humor her. But now that the baby was born there was no way to dance around or sugarcoat it anymore. Really, it was all just fat.

"Might be hormones," the man on the couch says. "From what I've heard, they can hit pretty hard. Maybe she's postpartum."

"No." Raymond stares at the darkness beyond the living room window, a hole created by a missing streetlight. "It started before."

So many things he expected to get better have only gotten worse since the baby was born. Every now and then his wife just seems to go berserk.

Just this morning, in fact, they had a terrible argument due to what Mathilda called his "arrogant assumptions" as to what constituted trash. He'd been going through old boxes in the attic and all he'd done was tell her the truth: that he'd never really noticed how much junk they'd accumulated in the course of their lives together until he had the opportunity to go through it all piece by piece.

"Look at all this crap. What do you even need it for?"

At first Mathilda shrugged and muttered something about emergency supplies, like a flashlight or flares. Things you didn't use every day but never knew when they might come in handy. It was only later that she told him it was "none of his business," that he had no right to ask her to justify things that, by his own admission, he'd never even noticed before. Things that belonged tucked and hidden in some drawer. Which was why she'd gotten so hysterical when she'd looked out the kitchen window and realized he'd taken it upon himself to set those things on the curb.

The whole city is like that now: Excavated memories dipped in a fine layer of silt. Doors left hanging open, soiled curtains floating stiffly through broken windows, watermarks cutting into the sides of houses like bruises on a thigh. Yet somehow Raymond and Mathilda are among the lucky ones. The truth is they are uptown and by the river and therefore have suffered very little structural damage.

Right now Mathilda is standing naked in the bathroom, staring at her own fleshy behind. She looks as though she forgot where she put it and then just stumbled on it by accident after not seeing it for years. There is something about her expression that is too dull and glossy-eyed to be properly called startled. But she can't seem to tear her eyes away—never mind that they have guests. For the moment Mathilda is stuck, all twisted around, rubbernecking her own ass.

Through the door she can hear the muffled sound of voices coming from the living room, her husband talking to the young couple that bought the house next door.

"I try to tell her she was too skinny before, that I like women with a little meat on their bones, a little junk in the trunk. But she doesn't seem to care."

"It's hard for women," the woman says. "Just look at the media these days. We're under so much pressure, not just to be perfect but to look perfect too."

"Oh, she knows all about that. Her roommate in college was bulimic."

"Somehow it seems to hit women who should know better the hardest. College-educated, professional women, the ones who look like they've got it all together. They're the ones who suffer the most." The woman smiles consolingly. "I imagine that when you reach a certain age it can really start to chip away at your self-esteem."

Mathilda listens, trying to figure out why her new neighbors irritate her so much. Until their arrival a few months before, most of the new people in the city had fallen into easily identifiable groups. First there are the witnesses, those motivated by reasons both personal and professional to see the devastation of the hurricane up close. The ones she watched as part of the small, observant congregation that formed the second line trailing after the marching band that paraded through the rubble of downtown a few days after their return. They walked along the empty roads, cameras clicking as they stumbled over the cracked sidewalks, broken tree branches, and streetlights that lay overturned at what seemed to be every intersection.

Then there are the Mexican and Brazilian men who came to do construction. They hammer on roofs, dump plaster on the pavement, and stare back at her with stoic expressions whenever she passes them on the street. At night they sleep in abandoned cars in the parking lot of a boarded-up Popeyes Chicken franchise and in the morning they stand in listless circles in front of the gas station on Claiborne, waiting to be crowded into the back of pickup trucks with Texas license plates.

Finally, there are the activists who have set up camp in various locations around the city, offering free meals and Shiatsu massages beneath a large white tent in City Park. Down in the neighborhood of Tremé they're staging rallies near St. Augustine, the oldest Black Catholic church in the city, which, though it suffered little damage during the storm, has been slated for closure due to "lack of attendance." And just a few days ago, when she and Raymond took two out-of-town visitors on a tour of the muted sandstorm that was the Ninth Ward, the only sign of life was a tall, dreadlocked teenager stepping out of a small lean-to, ducking as he passed beneath a hand-painted banner that read "Common Ground."

The new neighbors are too white to be day laborers, too well-scrubbed to be activists, too content with the narrow confines of "the sliver by the river," that uptown strip of high ground that borders the Mississippi, to be witnesses. When asked, they told her that they were from Virginia but spent part of their honeymoon here and visited often; they had good friends who attended law school at Tulane. When the storm hit they realized they wanted to invest in the city's future. It was as simple as that.

"One thing about all that's happened," she hears Raymond say. "It makes you realize what's important. The stuff we lost, they were just things. You know? Just surface. Because then I think, my wife had a baby. What could be more beautiful than that?"

Mathilda slips into her bra and panties. *Just don't start talking about tiger stripes*, she thinks. *You fucking idiot.*

"Even the stretch marks. I mean you should see them." Raymond sets his glass down on the coffee table and makes a gesture with his hands, like he is pulling on a silken thread, so delicate and fine he has to squint to see it. "They're like these thin, shiny, tiger-print slashes running up and down her hips and thighs. She hates them, of course. But I actually think they're sexy."

"That's so wonderful," the woman says. "I can't tell you how refreshing it is to meet a man who really appreciates the changes a woman's body goes through."

Mathilda looks at a pair of blue velvet pants salvaged from the trash heap earlier in the day. She wonders if it is possible that she simply misses her old neighbor, a depressive photographer who drank too much and lived alone with a rescued pit bull named Mollie. Too moody, too much of an alcoholic to hold down steady work, he talked about moving for years and finally resolved to put his house on the market just six months before the levees broke. But it was only after, when the National Guard was patrolling the streets in Humvees with rifles drawn, that he got anything approaching what he considered "a credible offer."

The house on the other side is, in contrast, still empty. The

Wilsons—a veteran of World War II and his wife—are in Arkansas now, staying with a nephew. They lived in the house on the corner for more than fifty years, having survived both Hurricane Betsy and the so-called period of white flight in the 1970s, when the middle class split in two, the whites heading west and the Blacks moving east. The day their son came to pack up their things he confessed that they were miserable in Arkansas, but the lack of emergency medical care in the city still prohibited their return.

Of course, none of that is the new neighbors' fault. Mathilda wonders: Does she hold it against them somehow, perhaps subconsciously? Is she really that petty?

No, of course not, she thinks. Mostly what bothers her, she's almost certain, is the stink.

"What I mean is, for me, it's all good," Raymond says. "I thought she looked beautiful before, but really, she looks even better to me now."

"Sure—it's a natural process, right?" the woman says. "These changes are inevitable, so we might as well embrace them."

The man on the couch pushes a pair of wire-rimmed glasses up the bridge of his nose. He's wearing an oxford shirt and khaki pants. A thick gold watch is balanced around his left wrist, which he checks. He smiles, then turns to the woman next to him and pats her on the knee. "Don't worry, honey. I'm sure that when we make the decision to have children, I'll find it sexy too."

"Sure," Raymond says. He reaches for the bottle and pours himself another glass. "Most men like a little ass."

A drawer slams shut in the bathroom and, still holding the wine bottle aloft, Raymond looks at the startled faces of the couple seated across from him. It occurs to him that he has forgotten their names. He has been discussing intimate details of his wife's anatomy with near strangers, people he barely knows. For a moment he feels confused, drifting in a sea of self-doubt. Then a wave of lucidity washes over him, their names coming back like life buoys in the midst of his own disorientation.

Brian and Tandy, Raymond thinks. *And they stink.*

"She should be out"—he smiles—"any minute now."

Mathilda steps into a pair of blue velvet pants. Everything is fine until she gets them halfway up her thigh, but after that all bets are off. The stretchy material abandons its promise and cuts into her flesh like those rubber bands her mother used to warn her not to wrap around her fingers as a child. She wiggles, shakes, and insists until at last they seem to come to an agreement. She stands in front of the mirror with her zipper hanging down and clutches the metal snaps together in the fist of her left hand.

She drops to her knees, lies down on the floor, and flaps her legs open and closed like a child making snow angels. Very slowly the material works its way over her hips. She sucks in her stomach and holds her breath, fingers straining to keep their grip on metal snaps that resist each other like magnetic pieces with like charges.

Finally the snaps collapse on top of one another, the clicking sound merging with her exhausted exhalation. Still flat on her back, she reaches down and yanks the zipper over her pubic bone, wincing against an ancient memory of a time in high school when, in the course of a similar maneuver, she accidentally snagged some hair.

"I always thought it was easier for Black women," Tandy says. "I mean, that's what you always hear. You know: different standards of beauty. Like with J.Lo and all those girls in the hip-hop videos."

Raymond smiles. *Bitch*, he thinks. Then he thinks: *What the fuck is she doing in there anyway?* Mathilda is the one who asked him to invite them over. Insisted on it, in fact. And then she locks herself in the bathroom, abandoning him to the snow and ice of chitchat. Leaving him alone to pick up the slack. And not for the first time either.

"Well, now you see, Tandy, that's a problem in this country—trying to separate issues of race and class."

He sets his glass down and reaches for one of the hors d'oeuvres that Mathilda set out on a small tray before their guests arrived. Upon biting into it, he is dismayed to discover they have not been given sufficient time to thaw.

"It's like with tipping," he says. "You always hear that Black people don't tip when really it's people who aren't used to eating in certain types of restaurants who don't leave tips. Where I come from, most people are always so careful about giving people their proper due that I never really understood that particular stereotype until I started waiting tables to pay my way through college. You see, my mother was a woman who believed in people paying their due, so that's just how I was raised." He smiled. "But really, it's like saying Black people are somehow genetically preprogrammed to have no class."

Mathilda looks at herself in the mirror. She still remembers the first time she tried the pants on, what a comfort it was to slide so easily into a size four. Those were the days when she was still young and streamlined, when very little was left to chance.

"Similarly, my wife is not some dancer shaking her ass in a music video," Raymond says. "She went to UC Berkeley, for crissakes."

"Well, I certainly didn't mean to imply—"

"No, of course not, Tandy. I realize that, of course."

Mathilda turns around in the mirror, thinking about the old days when everything was tight and flat. Pants had to be cut just right, not so loose that they sagged in the back, but not so tight that they became what her college roommate correctly identified, in her frequent evaluations of other girls' wardrobes, as "unfortunate ass smashers." Her college roommate, clucking her tongue at other girls' various failed attempts to impress or inspire envy. Her college roommate, whom she hasn't seen since graduation and hasn't thought about in years. Everyone said they looked like sisters. But then they had a falling-out in the middle of their junior year and never spoke to each other again. And now it was all so long ago she can barely remember why.

What she did remember was turning around and around in the dressing room mirror the day she bought the pants, while her roommate stared with her mouth ajar and heavy-lidded eyes full of that hot mixture of jealousy and desire that was the mask her friend always wore when she pictured her in her mind.

Look what I found, Mathilda said.

"I hope you didn't take that the wrong way," Brian says, coming to Tandy's defense. "I mean, it's not really a race thing, now is it? You have to admit there are differences, that some things are cultural."

"Sure." Raymond nods. "My concern is that these types of preconceptions can sometimes prevent people from getting the help they need."

Mathilda stares at the gelatinous rolls of fat dribbling over her waistband, the soft mounds of flesh crouched in cowering folds below her navel. Love has made her lethargic, she thinks. Has dulled the sharp edge of her vigilance. She leans over the toilet and shoves two fingers down her throat.

"You take that girl I mentioned before," Raymond says. "My wife's college roommate. It just so happens that she was Black. Or like my wife anyway. You know: halfsies. Her father was African, a surgeon and very successful entrepreneur. He invented something called the Fulani pouch, which apparently revolutionized gastric bypass surgery."

"Is that a tummy tuck?" Brian asks.

Tandy pats Brian's hand. "No, honey. A stomach staple. Makes your stomach half the size. So you can't eat."

"That's right, Tandy. And because of his invention, this girl was quite wealthy. She grew up in Beverly Hills, California, soaking up all the complexes and problems you might normally associate with rich white girls. You should have seen her back in school. While some of us were working our asses off to pay for college, there she was, partying and dancing all night. Sleeping with men twice her age that she picked up at bars, getting high, snorting coke . . . always the life of the party, no matter what."

Raymond shakes his head: "All the things going on in this world, but for her it was all just surface. Of course, it goes without saying that she was painfully neurotic about being thin. You might think that given her father's vocation, his particular clientele, he would have had some insight into his daughter's condition. But no, he just let her run wild and, for as long as was humanly possible, everyone acted like there wasn't a problem. When I met her as a freshman she weighed 130 pounds. By the time she was a junior, she was down to ninety-two."

"How tragic," Tandy says.

"The saddest part was that even after she was asked to leave school they put her in a treatment facility for methamphetamine. They thought she was addicted to drugs just because she took them. But, again, that was just surface. Really, they were appetite suppressants—a means to an end. The only thing that girl was addicted to was hunger."

Another drawer slams shut in the bathroom, but this time Raymond ignores it. He stares at his new neighbors.

It's the stink, he thinks. That's the reason his wife hasn't come out yet. And, really, it's not so much Brian and Tandy themselves as the garbage they leave behind. They purchased the house as some sort of investment and fly in for a few days at a time to initiate a flurry of activity on the roof. In the afternoons sometimes they host gatherings in the backyard, what appear from the living room window to be simple garden parties, but which Raymond is convinced are in fact meetings with other potential investors like themselves. Men in suits drinking chardonnay from plastic cups, women in pink and yellow sundresses eating crawfish served on paper plates. *People with money*. Clearly, they have some larger plan for the neighborhood that they have not elected to share as yet. And then, when the parties are over, they stuff all their garbage into large plastic bags they stack neatly along the curb in front of the house before they take off again, sometimes for weeks at a time. All without realizing, he assumes, that garbage is only being collected once a week these days. If they are lucky.

A *simple lapse of judgment*, he assured Mathilda the last time it happened. He tried to get her to look at the big picture: Brian and Tandy are contributing to the city's footprint, a term he had never heard before the hurricane hit, but which now gets bandied about with great frequency. The sudden arrival of Brian and Tandy is a good sign that things will get better, eventually. A little stink, relatively slight, all things considered, is only to be expected during a period of readjustment.

Mathilda flushes the toilet, pushes through a door, and walks to the bedroom to check on the baby. She reaches down and hoists the still-sleeping child to her chest, then stares out the window above the crib. She sees heaps of splintered wood set out on the corner, battered roofs covered in bright blue tarp, a spray-painted sign smeared over the front of the house across the street that reads "DO NOT STEAL BRICK." She wonders if Raymond realizes that, for all his pity, her college roommate always despised him. *Get rid of him*, she used to whisper, even as she smiled and waved.

"So you're an architect, right, Brian?" she hears Raymond say.

"That's right."

"Well, I imagine this must be a pretty interesting place to be right now, what with all the construction going on."

"Of course, a very exciting time. And what about you two? Are you planning to stay?"

"I think we're like a lot of people right now. Still weighing our options. My job is here and given everything that's happened, I consider myself lucky to have one at all."

"Were a lot of people at Bedlam and Stern let go?"

"Sure. They had to get rid of overlap and nonessential person-nel. A lot of people had to be purged. Of course, people are always surprised to find out that they are nonessential when parameters are redrawn."

"Yes, the truth hurts. But what can you do? Everybody's still in crisis mode, no choice but to trim the fat. Sometimes it takes a natural disaster to make people accept that."

"But it wasn't natural at all," Raymond says. "Remember? The levees broke. . . ."

He looks up as Mathilda appears in the hallway, her arms wrapped around a still-sleeping child. He sees the loose skin of her stomach sagging over her waistband. Flesh of her thighs bunched up in unnat-ural folds. Strained grip of blue velvet seams visibly splitting around her hips . . .

All dressed up out of spite in a pair of too-tight pants.

"Don't you look nice," he says between clenched teeth.

• • •

IT WAS THE INSURANCE COMPANY that asked them to go through every-thing that was damaged or lost, to come up with a plausible estimate of its worth. Before that they always assumed they had more to lose.

Crack Babies!

(2006)

"First of all, there's no such thing," Mr. Johnson said. I was fourteen years old and in the ninth grade. We were supposed to be reviewing for the math test on Monday—that's all I knew when I walked through the classroom door.

"The crack baby epidemic was a myth propagated by a right-wing corporate media as a moral justification for a racist drug policy. I want you to write that down. Go ahead. Take your seats, open your notebooks, and pick up your pens."

I removed the cap from a black BIC and stared at Mr. Johnson. He was wearing a green tie, yellow shirt, and thick glasses with black plastic frames. It looked like he styled his hair by combing it out into a dry frizzy Afro and then using a wet club brush to smooth it back down. I just assumed he didn't have a family because I couldn't imagine anybody who really loved him letting him walk out the front door with his hair looking like that.

"The war on drugs was nothing more than a smear campaign against working-class people, both Black and white," Mr. Johnson said. "You see, crack was always a poor man's cocaine. Real cocaine was for rich people. So they weren't going after drugs. They were going after the poor."

I wrote that down.

Behind me, I could already hear some kids snickering in the back row:

A propa-who?

How you spelling epidemic?

Is this going to be on the test, Mr. Johnson?

There was a knock on the classroom door. Mr. Johnson opened it just wide enough so that the hall monitor could pass him a note. He glanced at it for a moment and then shut the door and crumpled the note into a ball. He threw it into the wastebasket next to his desk.

"Don't believe the hype," Mr. Johnson told us. "Do you children realize that the United States of America, this so-called land of freedom, is home to the largest prison-industrial complex in the world? That during the short period of time between when most of you were born and today the prison population in this country has grown over five hundred percent? And who do you think most of these people sitting in jail are? Do you even realize how many of these so-called criminals are petty thieves and drug addicts, not the dangerous thugs you always see splashed across the media? Are they receiving treatment? Are they being rehabilitated? They are not. Write that down."

I wrote it down.

Are we still having the test on Monday?

He walked around and sat on the front of his desk and looked at us.

"Now I want you to tell me the truth. How many of you in here grew up without fathers in the home? Come on, now, don't be ashamed. . . . Do you know that I am not at all surprised to see so many hands raised?

"And how many of you have fathers or uncles or brothers in jail? Tell the truth, now."

Bertha? Where are you going?

"It's all right. She'll be all right."

What's she crying for?

"I know it's painful to talk about, but I want you to know that you are not alone."

What the fuck is this shit, Mr. Johnson?

"I feel sorry for you children, and that is the truth. You've been told so many lies about your fathers and brothers, about your mothers and sisters—about yourselves. When it's the prison system that is the cause of so much despair. An entire generation, they said, being born beyond repair. And believe it or not, that was you."

Me? What you say? I'm not no damn crack baby.

We put down our pens.

"I want you to look around you. I want you to take a good long look at your fellow accused. I want you to understand that when you walk outside this classroom, every day of your life is open combat against the lies that have been told about you, the things you have been taught to believe—some of those things right here, at this very school."

A bell rang.

"Now. As some of you may be aware, I have been asked to take a leave of absence."

You're leaving, Mr. Johnson? Where are you going?

"That means I won't be here when you come back to class on Monday."

What about the test, Mr. Johnson?

"This is your test, Tonya," Mr. Johnson said. "Class dismissed."

Everybody put their pens away and stood up. We filed past him on our way out the door, nobody saying a word to him except for Olivia:

"That was real righteous, what you said just now, Mr. Johnson. Its about time someone said something real up in here. . . ."

I walked outside and looked around the yard until I found Bertha sitting on a bench near the fence, next to the crowd of kids waiting for the school buses to pull up to the curb. A whole group of us from class—me, Johnny, Sandra, Tonya, Tony, Theo, Ronnie, and Olivia—walked over to ask Bertha if she was okay.

"That man had no business talking about people's daddies like that," Bertha said. "It's just wrong."

"You heard him say he's leaving, anyhow. I bet you that's why. Can't be talking like that in a classroom."

"What was that about, anyway?" I asked.

Johnny shook his head. "I don't know. When we first walked in, T-Bone was making a joke about somebody being fucked up because his mama smoked too much crack and Mr. Johnson's eyes kind of lit up. Next thing I knew, he was going off about crack babies."

"He looked crazy to me," Tonya said. "Getting all agitated like that. And he didn't say a thing about the test on Monday."

"He's just trying to remind you that you got a lot on you just walking down the street," Olivia said. "Me? I thought it was about time we heard somebody say something righteous up in here."

"Well, it might have been more righteous if he had told us what was going to be on Monday's test," Tonya said. "I'm trying to graduate. How am I supposed to uplift myself when I don't even know what to study for the test?"

"He's stupid anyway, saying there's no such thing as crack babies. That's a lie," Bertha said. "My aunt's cousin has got one living in her house right now. Took her in when she was just a baby and the girl is still fucked in the head. You hear me? It's not the mama who raised her but my aunt's cousin who is a proper church-going woman—and still the girl peed her bed until she was twelve."

"Don't you think there's little white kids in the suburbs like that too?" Olivia said. "But they're hyperactive, they're dyslexic, all they got to do is pop a pill and it's fixed. No one calls them crack babies."

She walked away from us and took a seat on a nearby bench. For the next hour she sat by herself, headphones on and scribbling in her notebook, listening to the beats swirling around inside her head.

"I don't care what you say, Miss Olivia. Crack babies are no myth," Bertha said. She was so mad her left eye had started to twitch. "They're real, I tell you! Crack babies are real!"

Bertha had band practice. Sandra had to run home so she could babysit her brother while her mother was at work. Tonya and Tony drifted off with their arms draped around each other. Theo and Ronnie said something about going to the park to play basketball but Johnny didn't feel like going with them. We told them good-bye and sat together near the fence.

"That was weird," I said.

"Yeah." Johnny nodded.

The last school bus pulled up and a group of kids piled inside. We saw Mr. Johnson walk out a side door, coming from the principal's office.

"Bye-bye, Mr. Marcus Johnson," I said. But he was on the other side of the parking lot, so the only one who heard me was Johnny.

"You think maybe he knows what he was talking about?"

"What do you mean?"

"You think he's ever been to jail?"

We watched Mr. Johnson load his box into the trunk, then climb into a crappy blue Honda, with his funky-looking suit and his funky-looking hair.

"You think he knows Bertha's daddy?" Johnny said.

Then we started talking about something else.

Paulie Sparks

(2007)

1.

Paulie Sparks was coming to town. In fact, he was already here and waiting outside baggage claim and content to take the couch. When of course James should have asked his wife Mindy first, if only out of courtesy, to say nothing of respect. Making this just another example of the type of thing she meant.

"What type of thing?" James said. He looked around the living room, trying to find his car keys. He glanced at the coffee table, the top of the credenza, the arm of the sofa where their son, Franklin, sat watching TV. Then back at Mindy, whose eyes were welling up with tears.

"Come on now, Mindy. Don't be like that. He'll only be here for a few weeks at most."

He didn't understand why she was upset. Mindy knew the situation with Paulie, knew very well the man had nowhere else to go. She'd been standing right next to James the night of Judge Smith's mixer when Diego Jones pulled them both aside and said, "Paulie Sparks, remember him? From junior high?" Then proceeded to tell them the whole sad tale. How Paulie never graduated high school, never settled down or found his place, and finally never showed up for his aunt Josephine's funeral, which was odd when you considered how close they used to be. People got to whispering at the wake, and none of them were really surprised when it turned out he was stuck in jail somewhere in California.

"A three-strikes state," Diego said. Then described an embarrassing set of circumstances involving a gift certificate, a pizza parlor, and a teenaged cashier.

"It's that box cutter that did it," Diego explained, the box cutter being the weapon that had fallen out of Paulie's pocket as he took off with the stolen slice, making the incident a third felony assault.

Mindy was the one who'd asked James to look into it. He was a lawyer, after all; surely there was something he could do. So he'd made a few phone calls and managed to get ahold of the transcripts of Paulie's last trial. Dug deep through the rubble of Paulie's official record until he found, buried beneath years of drug use and drifting, a fifteen-year-old improper search and seizure that had initiated Paulie's decline.

"You should have asked me first, James. Why can't you just admit that?"

But he had admitted it. Hadn't he? And anyway it was not his fault. Because of course Paulie would want to come here, if only to thank him. After all those hours of pro bono work trying to get him out of jail, what should James have said? *I think it's okay, but let me check with my wife?*

"But why here, James? I mean, is it even safe?" Because in truth neither of them had seen Paulie in twenty years.

"What exactly are we supposed to do with him? When we're barely getting by as it is?"

James frowned. Barely getting by was a comfortable home in a nice, clean suburb. It was a backyard swimming pool, a cypress dinner table, a leather sofa, a flat-screen TV. James still remembered junior high, when he and Paulie both had to walk around town in hand-me-down clothes, duct tape holding together the soles of their shoes. But these days, apparently, barely getting by meant never knowing what it meant to make do.

"Never mind me but what about Franklin? Did you even stop to think about your son?"

James looked at his son, slack-jawed and staring as he gripped the remote, an overturned book bag lying at his feet. The boy's life was easy, a vast tapestry of creature comforts, full of things James never had as a child. To say nothing of Paulie Sparks.

"It just seems like you would at least *ask* before you invite a convicted felon into our home. . . ."

James squinted at his son. The TV, he realized, wasn't even on. The boy was just sitting there with his mouth hanging open, watching the two of them argue on a dark screen.

He looked back at Mindy.

Of course, he thought. *It's the boy.*

Because the only thing they couldn't afford was private school. Which in truth was something neither of them had even noticed until someone at the local public school made the mistake of implying that Franklin's current grades in math had nothing to do with a conflict with his teacher but rather the possibility that the boy was, perhaps, simply slow. Mindy had been in a funk about it ever since. Making all this subterfuge just the latest excuse to vent her frustration and rage.

Paulie Sparks has nothing to do with it—

And there, on the mantle, he finally spotted his keys.

"Don't worry about dinner."

James shut the door behind him. He stood on the porch and thought back to the night of Judge Smith's mixer, how in sync he and Mindy had felt then. After Diego told them about Paulie they'd stayed together for a long time, huddled in a corner of the judge's living room, discussing various conspiracies of injustice even as they contemplated their own relative comfort and the relative mildness of their own meager crimes.

He'd thought Mindy would be proud of him and walked to his car only vaguely aware that a lot had happened between that night and this one. The missed dinners, the arguments, the newspaper articles about graduation rates for African American boys in the public school system being shoved under his nose at the breakfast table. Yet in some ways there was only the inspiration of the night of the mixer and then the disappointment of this.

All the petty grievances of his day-to-day life with Mindy were just the blur that had passed in between. Actual memories were made of singular gestures, moments that defined you, what you had to hold on to when all was said and done. He wondered why Mindy couldn't understand that. Just like he wondered why, after fifteen years of marriage, she still behaved as if repeatedly startled to discover that he was a man of his word.

He backed out of his driveway, wound down a tree-lined street, and passed through the stone pillars that marked the entrance to their communal drive. As he merged onto the interstate he saw a sign he'd been looking for without knowing he was looking for it until he glanced up at a billboard and there it was. All at once he knew this moment was a triumph that no one could take away from him. He had righted an injustice; he had done the right thing; he alone was responsible for getting Paulie Sparks out of jail. All those unpaid hours spent alone in his office, struggling to pull some meaning from Paulie's case, had not been in vain.

"Get with the Now," the billboard said.

2.

This was the now Paulie Sparks wanted to get with: Senator Obama's airbrushed smile shining down from a billboard propped alongside

Route 1. It was the kind of smile that made Paulie think about statutes of limitations and the bright blue do-over of a brand-new day. It was the smiling promise of hope and renewal draped beneath the broad banner that bore the mantra of Obama's presidential campaign:

"Are You Ready for the New Positive?"

Are you, Paulie? Paulie wondered. *Because this is the Now you need.*

"I'm sorry? What did you say?"

Paulie looked at James hunched over the steering wheel as the two of them sped down the interstate. He nodded towards the billboard.

"Man," he said. "That motherfucker is everywhere."

"Hard to believe, isn't it?" James said. "I mean, can you imagine? A Black president? Of these United States?" He shook his head. "I guess it just goes to show how much things have changed. . . ."

James's voice trailed off. Paulie felt his friend's eyes trace a line along the scar that ran down the left side of Paulie's face before he caught himself and looked back at the road. It was the same look James had given him when he pulled up outside baggage claim, as he watched Paulie climb into the passenger seat of the car. Like he'd been expecting someone else.

Got this out in LA about five years ago, Paulie wanted to say but was waiting for James to ask about it first. It was awkward. They hadn't seen each other in twenty years, which meant they didn't really know each other anymore but thought they did. Or should. When here was the truth about scars: whatever pain they stood for had healed over long before. Paulie forgot they were there most of the time, until he saw them reflected in someone else's eyes.

Which brings us back to the matter of statutes of limitations, Paulie thought. He wondered: *Can a man consciously decide what memories he holds on to? Or is that really just an effect of his nature?*

"What did you say?"

This moment, for example, which reminded Paulie of something, yet was not something he could have foreseen. Somehow James, an old school friend, someone Paulie hadn't thought about in decades, found out about his situation and felt motivated to do something. And now here Paulie was. After all that time trying to figure out his next move, it turned out all Paulie had to do was be ready for it. Because just like that, everything changed.

So sometimes recognition is a form of forgetting.

"What was that?"

He smiled at James. "Man, I want you to know I'm not going to forget this. You hear me? I owe you, man. For real."

"I hear you."

Because you were there when I needed you, Paulie thought. *Let that be the important thing.*

"You know how you can pay me back, Paulie? Just live your life. I mean, what happened to you is so fucked up. But now you've got a second chance. I want you to put the past behind you and just go out there and live."

Paulie nodded. *Platitudes.* He looked out the window.

"I notice you haven't even asked me about how I wound up—"

"No. Listen, Paulie. Did you read what I wrote in that petition? Because it's not just a technicality as far as I'm concerned. Whatever happened after that first conviction is immaterial. You've served your time."

"But that's what I'm talking about. That first one." Paulie shook his head. "I was just a kid back then, although of course I didn't realize it at the time. Easy to manipulate. And say you got a situation where it seems like the best you can do is mop floors in some old man's bar and someone you trust says, do this for me. Says, easy money, you in, you out? All you got to do is move a freezer out of someone's garage and—"

James threw up his hand. "I really don't need to hear this. Truth? It's probably better if I don't."

Paulie nodded. He watched another billboard whiz by: Senator Obama's bright, clean smile balanced by the fixity of his own gaze. Yet somehow when you looked at the man's picture you saw the truth of things, all you needed to know, right there, in the senator's eyes.

Don't fuck with this.

"What did you say?"

For example: a couple of months before James contacted him, Paulie's aunt's voice had come creeping up behind him, stepped out of some shadowless wall to speak truth to the craving of Paulie's heart.

"Ain't nobody been by to visit me. They forgot the promises they made you a long time ago. You should have been here for my funeral."

Aunt Josephine said other things too, he could hear them clear as day.

"You coming up out of this, Paulie. And when you do, I want you to think. You hear me? I want you to do the right thing."

And somehow he'd known exactly what she meant.

He turned back to James. "Hey. Whadaya say we stop by Henry's Bar?"

"You mean now?" James shrugged. "Why not? I'm in no hurry to get home, that's for sure. . . ."

Paulie nodded. *Do me this solid.* You shake hands with someone, you bump fists. Maybe fifteen years ago someone says, "Trust me," and puts you on a bus headed out of town. They tell you they're just looking out for you, that they'll take care of your aunt and hold your money while you're gone and then send for you as soon as it's safe to come home. And because you got heart you hold on to that moment, you play it back in your mind for years. But how could you know if the memory you were holding on to was the right one? How could you really know who would be there for you in this life, or even why?

So the important thing is to be ready.

"What did you say, man?"

"Nothing, James. Never mind."

They pulled into the parking lot of Henry's Bar. They pushed through the front door, and at first everything was just like Paulie remembered, dark and glittery-eyed, full of smoke and music and loud-talking people, all of whom looked familiar, although in truth he did not recognize a single one.

"Paulie Sparks? Is that you?"

Paulie squinted past the bar and saw Henry sitting in a booth by the jukebox, wearing the same straw hat and flashy suit he used to wear when Paulie worked there. It wasn't until he stood up that Paulie saw Henry was smaller than he'd remembered; for a moment he could have been any bony old man, frail and flabby-armed, shuffling across the floor.

Henry said, "If you aren't a sight for sore eyes," and put a hand on Paulie's shoulder. Paulie realized he'd never taken the time to imagine what this moment would actually feel like, although he'd memorized the look of it many times.

This was all wrong.

Henry turned to James. "Well, I guess you really did it. Got the boy back home, just like you said you would. You must be some good lawyer."

"I try." James smiled.

Henry shook his head. He looked Paulie up and down, eyes rolling right over Paulie's scar as if he hadn't seen it. "Why, you haven't changed a bit."

Which, of course, was all wrong too.

"And you said it couldn't be done," James said.

Then Henry turned towards the bar and shouted, "Eddie? What's wrong with you? Give this man a drink."

Paulie looked up at a squat, heavyset man standing behind the bar. The last time he'd seen Eddie he was still a scrawny kid who ran the dishwasher while Paulie mopped the floors; fifteen years later it was like he'd fleshed out to the point where even the bones of his face had swollen. Eddie set three shot glasses and a bottle of whiskey on the table and gave Paulie a quick nod.

"Long time no see."

Motherfucker, I remember you, Paulie thought. He didn't even realize he'd said it out loud until he looked around the table and saw everybody staring. So now the truth was out, that sometimes Paulie talked to himself, more and more lately, and it was just like the scar in that usually he didn't even know he was doing it until he looked up and saw somebody watching him. So he was irritated by having to think about that. He turned to Henry and said, "Why don't we quit all this fucking around?" which came out loud and not sounding like he'd imagined or wanted it to. But really he shouldn't have had to say anything at all. Because Henry should have been the one to say it. Just like he should have come to tell Paulie about his aunt or been the one to figure out how to get him out of jail. Not James. *Who the fuck was James?*

"Is something the matter?" James said.

Henry shook his head. "No. Now, look, there's no problem we can't solve. It's just been a long time. Paulie, why don't you come in my office for a minute? So we can talk."

Paulie nodded. He stood up and smiled like somehow this was all a private joke between him and Henry.

This won't take long, James, man, so why don't you just relax, stay here and enjoy your drink because I got this.

They walked to Henry's office. Henry shut the door and Paulie took a seat in front of his desk.

"I want you to know how sorry I was about your aunt," Henry said. "And you're right, I should have called you. But seriously? After you got arrested that last time I really didn't know how to get ahold of you. And then when I did so much time had passed; I guess I didn't know what to say. . . ."

While he was talking Paulie looked around the room. He thought about how nervous he used to feel when he worked there, every time he pushed through Henry's door on Friday nights to pick up his check. He thought about how impressive Henry always looked sitting behind his desk with those big flashy rings on his fingers as he counted out the night's receipts. He thought about how one time he'd pushed through that door and found Henry staring back at him with his fist wrapped around a fat stack of dollar bills. Paulie had been so distracted by the shine of all those rings that it had taken a moment to understand Henry was asking him if he wanted the chance to make some real money.

Paulie remembered how bad he'd felt when it all went wrong and then how relieved he'd been when he found out that the security guard he'd hit with that crowbar was going to be all right. And he remembered what had come after that, the very last time he'd been in Henry's office. How he'd sat in the same chair he was sitting in now, slobbering and crying all over himself until he looked up and saw Eddie standing by the door. It was the disgust in Eddie's eyes that finally made Paulie pull himself together. He'd wiped his face and then, when he'd looked back at Henry's hands, he'd seen they were holding out a bus ticket.

Paulie looked at Henry's hands now, empty and flailing as he stuttered and stammered and tried to explain. It occurred to Paulie that Henry was still wearing the same rings but somehow nothing about Henry or his bar seemed to shine the way it used to. For fifteen years Paulie had held on to an image of Henry's glittery fingers holding his money and smoothing things over and making sure his aunt was okay. For fifteen years Paulie had lived his life stuck in a numb daze of trying to make himself scarce until it was safe to come home, while everything around him seemed to whiz by in a confused blur. And it occurred to him that what made this particular moment memorable was not disappointment. Because Henry hadn't changed at all. It was the realization that somehow, without even being aware that it was happening, the one who had changed was Paulie Sparks.

"Where the fuck is my money?" Paulie said.

Henry shook his head and told him flat-out he didn't have it.

3.

At two the next morning James was back at home and lying in bed next to Mindy. He'd had four drinks by the time Paulie walked out of Henry's office alone. Then the two of them left the bar and spent the next three hours sitting in the car, talking. He figured it had taken about twenty minutes of listening to Paulie ramble incoherently for him to accept that his old friend might have mental problems. The next half hour had been spent going over the shrill scolding Mindy had given him on his way out the door. He realized that maybe he'd misinterpreted what she'd been trying to say. Maybe she'd meant that getting Paulie out of jail was just the first step of what would probably be a long climb. Because, all platitudes aside, Paulie was clearly traumatized by whatever he'd been through over the past two decades. He needed help, professional help, and more of it than they themselves could provide. He'd spent the next two hours trying to assure himself that Paulie was not in fact dangerous and that therefore it was safe to bring him home.

Now he felt overwhelmed by the desire to apologize. So he put his hand on Mindy's shoulder and pushed and pushed until finally she opened her eyes.

"What happened? What's wrong?"

"No, nothing's wrong. I just want to tell you . . . I'm sorry."

"Sorry for what?" She squinted. "You've been drinking, haven't you?"

James stared at his wife. He could feel a sad coldness creeping in between them yet again and struggled for a moment, trying to figure out what to say.

"It's the boy," he said finally. "I want you to call that school tomorrow and see if they still have a place for him."

"But you told me it was too expensive."

"I was wrong," he said. "I know I've been distracted lately because of Paulie's case. But that's over. Franklin's our son and we have to do whatever is necessary to ensure his future. I see that now. His education is too important to let this opportunity pass by. We'll find a way."

"Really?"

"Of course."

A fresh start, a new day. The right words, right there all along.

"Oh James—"

Welcome home.

It wasn't until five hours later, when he walked to the kitchen and saw Mindy dressed for work and standing by the stove, that it occurred to James that everything he'd told her while they were lying in bed together had been a lie. They didn't have the money to afford private school; Paulie's apparent mental problems did nothing to change that. What had he been thinking?

"Morning." She smiled. She poured him a glass of orange juice, set it on the table, and kissed him on the cheek. "I invited a few friends over tonight. I hope you don't mind. I thought maybe it would be good for Paulie to meet some people."

He said nothing as she reached for her keys.

"Are you all right?"

"Yes," he said. "Everything is fine."

He watched her walk out the door, already wondering how long it would take her to forget the things he'd told her, to forgive him for all the false promises he'd made the night before. . . .

Out of nowhere, a paper bag full of money landed on his plate.

4.

"That's your cut," Paulie said.

James looked at the bag and then up at Paulie, who stood over the kitchen table.

"I'm sorry? My what?"

"Your cut." Paulie smiled. "What'd I tell you last night? I owe you, man. Anyhow, I figure it's the least I could do."

James peeked inside. The bag was indeed full of money. Not pretty money either. Crumpled bills, clearly wrenched from unwilling fingers. It constituted, James realized, a confession of some sort. He shut the bag.

"Count it," Paulie said.

"I don't want to count it. Where did you get this?"

"Henry's been holding it for me. I'll admit there was a bit of confusion as to the fact that that was what he was doing. But we got it all straightened out."

James shook his head. "I can't accept this."

Paulie frowned. "Don't be a fool. It's a victimless crime. Matter of fact, if there is a victim, it's me."

"But I can't—"

"Oh, you're going to take it, all right," Paulie said. "Because unlike some folks, I am a man of my word. A man of principle. And it turns out my discipline is very strict."

Paulie poured himself a glass of orange juice, drank it, then set his glass down and went out, he said, to find his own apartment in town.

James called in sick at work that morning because he was sick. He took the bag of money and drove to the municipal park, then sat in his car and tried to figure out what he should do. At some point he got out, walked to a newsstand, and bought the morning paper. It took a while to find what he was looking for, but as soon as he did he knew what was true. According to the metro section, longtime bar owner Henry Moore had OD'd last night.

James walked back to his car. He got in the driver's seat and looked at the bag of money sitting on the passenger side. He opened it and peeked inside, eyes scanning the denominations of the bills, most of which were hundreds.

He thought about the promise he'd made to his wife.

He picked up the paper again and turned back to the metro section. The brief article pointed out that Henry was seventy-eight and had a long history of drug abuse. Over the course of his career, there had been several arrests for drug possession and one court-mandated stint in rehab. Best remembered as the younger brother of Leon Moore, the controversial founder of the Moore Center for Creative Unity. Henry's Bar had been a longtime landmark of the city's south side, the future of which was now uncertain. He would be missed.

James set the paper down. He looked at the bag of money. Then he shut his eyes and, because sometimes recognition is a form of forgetting, began to assess the various ways it could be argued that he'd done nothing wrong.

5.

The night before Paulie had tried to explain it to James. That he was a hard-angled man, by which he meant he was simply a man of his word. That he'd lived with himself long enough to know he was capable of making utterly foolish choices, which was why, for a long time, he'd tried to give himself no choice. That there were certain things he'd done in the past that he still felt bad about, things that, if he was honest, he knew himself to be more than capable of doing again.

That his truest aspiration had always been to some day open a bar like Henry's and live the life of an independent businessman. That he was halfway through a correspondence course in business administration; he meant business, which was not just an idler's wishing and dreaming. It was knowledge and a clearly defined skill set.

That atonement was a necessary precondition of reconciliation. That reparations and retaliation were not at all the same thing. That hope, while predicated on faith, was also mediated by experience. There were numerous examples of situations Paulie had found himself in where others had doubted his basic loyalty and he had pretty much startled them all with his ability to surpass expectations, both reasonable and unreasonable.

That, if given this chance to start over and a little capital, he was positive he could not merely survive this world but thrive in it. Because he was free now, and what's more, he was ready for it.

"What?"

"What?"

A hard-angled man unleashed back upon the world. *For this*, Paulie Sparks thought, *for each and every one of us, is surely the dawning of a brand-new day.*

Acknowledgments

This book was written over several years and benefited from the wisdom and insight of a great many people. Among the many deserving of gratitude for their contributions to its creation are Toni Morrison, Barbara Christian, Cornel West, Alison Warner, Jacqueline Hubbard, Peter C. Williams, Minnie C. Williams, Haven Hubbard, ZZ Packer, Stewart O'Nan, Mat Johnson, Mary Gaitskill, Jesse Lee Kercheval, Judith Mitchell, Lorrie Moore, Shoshana Vogel, Daryl Chou, Zachary Lazar, Charles Williams, and Jackie Williams. I also would like to thank my agent, Ayesha Pande, and my editor, Patrik Henry Bass, for their belief in this project, and everyone at HarperCollins who contributed to making this book a reality.

Significant portions of this book were written during residencies at Hedgebrook, Camargo, and A Studio in the Woods. I thank them for providing much-needed time and support.

A special thank-you to Christopher Dunn and my three children, who are a continual source of inspiration: Isa Yasmin-Gonzalez, Joaquin Hubbard Dunn, and Ze Hubbard Dunn.

About the Author

Ladee Hubbard is the author of the novels *The Rib King* and *The Talented Ribkins*. Her short fiction has appeared in the *Oxford American*, *Guernica*, the *Virginia Quarterly Review*, and *Callaloo*, among other publications. She is a recipient of an Ernest J. Gaines Award for Literary Excellence, a Hurston/Wright Legacy Award for Debut Fiction, and a Rona Jaffe Foundation Writers' Award. She has received fellowships from the Radcliffe Institute for Advanced Study, the American Academy in Berlin, MacDowell, and Hedgebrook, among other organizations. Born in Massachusetts and raised in the US Virgin Islands and Florida, she currently lives in New Orleans.